ADVANCE PRAISE FOR
A SMALL REVOLUTION

"We've all wondered what it's like inside the rooms where the horrors unfold. Jimin Han's relentless, timely *A Small Revolution* grabs you by the collar and pulls you inside, then back through her sympathetic character's history to answer that question: How does a good girl end up inside a brutal disaster? How does young love become a mirage of political activism—and accident become hostage-taking and murder? Open the book; remember to breathe."

—Gwendolen Gross, author of *When She Was Gone* and
The Orphan Sister

"On the heels of South Korea's 1980s-era pro-democracy uprisings, Jimin Han's gripping debut novel, *A Small Revolution*, explores the volatile space between love and loss, desperation and deed."

—Julie Iromuanya, author of *Mr. and Mrs. Doctor*, a finalist for the 2016 PEN/Faulkner Award and the 2016 PEN/Robert W. Bingham Prize for Debut Fiction

"Jimin Han's debut novel, *A Small Revolution*, is a riveting and mysterious tale of young love, political intrigue, family secrets, and dangerous obsession rendered in prose so gripping I couldn't put it down."

—Joy Castro, author of *The Truth Book* and *Hell or High Water*

A SMALL
REVOLUTION

A SMALL REVOLUTION

A NOVEL

JIMIN HAN

Little a

Published by Little A, New York

www.apub.com

Amazon, the Amazon logo, and Little A are trademarks of Amazon.com, Inc., or its affiliates.

"Even the Birds Are Leaving the World" by Hwang Chiu, in *Modern Korean Literature: An Anthology*, ed. Peter H. Lee (Honolulu: University of Hawaii Press, 1990)

ISBN-13: 9781503939738 (hardcover)
ISBN-10: 1503939731 (hardcover)

ISBN-13: 9781503939721 (paperback)
ISBN-10: 1503939723 (paperback)

Cover design by Ginger Design

Printed in the United States of America

First edition

For my mother

AUTHOR'S NOTE

This book is a work of fiction. I owe much to firsthand accounts from family and friends and the many journalists and scholars who have written about Korea (among them Bruce Cumings, author of *Korea's Place in the Sun*, and Don Oberdorfer, author of *The Two Koreas*). The poem "Even the Birds Are Leaving the World" by Hwang Chiu particularly stood out for me in my readings and is mentioned in the novel itself. Any resemblance these characters have to real persons is unintentional. Since the phonetic spelling of Korean words and names has undergone a change since the time in which this novel is set, I've tried whenever possible to use the current spelling for the present-day reader.

1

A woman is running in a field of fallen leaves, and a man is running behind her. It's early enough in the morning for the sky to be gray and the trees to be black, early enough for me to hear only the sound of her breathing and his breathing, except for that moment when he gains on her, makes contact, and tackles her, and she lets out a high-pitched sound cut short as she hits the ground. This is the view I have from my open dorm window into the quadrangle of Weston College in the middle of Pennsylvania.

2

You told me once about a neighbor who had a border collie named Pirate. One day, you were outside early in the morning and saw two wild rabbits in your neighbor's yard, two small brown ones, and then you heard the back screen door slam and watched Pirate charge across the grass toward those rabbits. One took off for the bushes on the periphery, and Pirate pursued it while the other stayed absolutely still, like a statue, so still you questioned your own eyes. Was it a sculpture of a rabbit in the neighbor's yard? Pirate trotted out of the bushes, having given up the chase. He had never paid much attention to you before. But you walked toward the dog, calling him by name, rewarding him with long petting strokes, and backed away as slowly as you could, leading him away. When you looked up again, the statue was gone.

3

I remain at the dorm window. I stay, even when I see him stand her up and drag her stumbling by the back of her coat. He turns, retracing his steps, searching the ground, and then picks up something he had dropped earlier. He hoists it up and begins to walk forward again, keeping his other hand on the woman's coat and yanking her along. I stay, even when I know he is coming for me, even when I can see clearly that it is your friend Lloyd. I stay because the woman is someone I know well, and in his hand is a shotgun.

4

The screams in the hallway launch me toward the phone. I dial 911, and someone on the other end says, "What's your emergency?"

I think I'm saying, Come now, please, but a voice on the other end says, "Is someone there? I can't hear you. Can you tell me what's happening?"

"Yoona!" It's Daiyu shrieking in the hall. I drop the phone and run to the door and open it.

There are mud splats on her face. Her black hair a squashed nest. Daiyu Chu is a friend of mine from a dorm across campus. There are grass stains on the knees of her pink flannel pajamas. Her blue sweatshirt with the round Weston College logo is smeared with damp patches. Lloyd appears beside her. He's got a leer on his face, and his hair is wet, as if he has been caught in the rain.

"Yoona, he's crazy," Daiyu sobs. I can't help but step back, and he pushes her into the room. Daiyu scrambles toward the wall by my bed, moving as far from him as she can get, and hides her face in her hands. "What's—" is the only word I can say as Lloyd turns, still in the doorway, and raises a shotgun into the hall. More screams, and people scatter, and I hear Heather's voice. "Yoona, you okay?"

Heather Connelly has a room next to mine. Instead of fleeing, she's coming. "Don't!" I call out but Lloyd grabs her by the sleeve of her terry-cloth robe, and Heather reaches for Faye Taverson to save herself as if she is falling off a pier, and Faye is caught off guard, and Heather and Faye are reeled into the room.

Lloyd kicks the door closed. And someone pounds on it from the other side. A voice comes through, calling for me. It's Joanna, the resident adviser.

GO AWAY. I'LL KILL THEM ALL, Lloyd explodes. He shoots the gun. His shoulder jerks back. And it's as if a grenade went off in the room. I crouch on the floor, my arms over my head. There's ringing in my ears.

There's no more pounding on the door after that. I'm aware of Daiyu wailing from the corner behind me and Faye huddled on the bed to my left saying, "Oh my god, oh my god," over and over again

3

and Heather telling everyone to be quiet from somewhere to my right. I've heard gunfire before, but something about this room, this space, is louder than anything I've heard.

The sirens, when they come, loop as if they're fading and then growing louder. Are they coming to rescue us, or is it for someone else?

STOP. Lloyd shouts as if his words are coming out of a body that is itself a gun. STOP. STOP. WHATEVER YOU'RE THINKING, STOP. I'LL MAKE ALL OF YOU STOP.

5

"Wait, Lloyd? My friend Lloyd?" you would say. "What's Lloyd got to do with this? He wouldn't have a gun. He wouldn't do this. I know Lloyd, our Lloyd from Korea? Lloyd, my friend Lloyd?" You wouldn't believe it. You'd refuse.

And I'd tell you I'm sorry. I'm sorry, I'm sorry.

"How'd he get to your college? What's he doing in your room?" you would say.

I'm trying to tell you.

Listen.

6

My life was simple when I was a child. I walked to school with my older sister. I joined after-school clubs. I went home and did my homework. Some days, after dinner, my father beat my mother. Not often. But there were days when that happened, and in between were the days it was about to.

7

My mother said, "Don't trust a man, ever." My sister said, "Don't trust anyone." My father said, "No one understands me in this house."

8

You understood me. You understood Lloyd and me. If you were here in this room, you'd know what to do. What am I forgetting? You said I was good at making lists. To-do lists, to-see lists, to-make-us-remember lists, to-figure-out-how-we-got-here lists. To-tell-you-why-I-could-never-see-you-again lists.

9

The sirens keep coming. Heather holds the palm of her hand to her cheek, and when she takes it away, there's blood. Behind her in the wall is a four-inch gash as if someone pounded a clawed hammer into it with five circular punctures below it. Buckshot pellets. I know this because my father collects guns.

"Does it hurt?" I say, and she says, "Is it bad?" I remove a pillow from its case and hand it to her. Lloyd is kicking the door in a rhythmic way, shuffling and pacing and kicking, hugging the shotgun to his chest. Is anyone going to come through that door and rescue us?

"Jesus, he's going to kill us," Faye says.

He runs at her, the shotgun raised like an axe. WHAT ARE YOU PLAN-NING BEHIND MY BACK?

I stand up. "Lloyd, what are you doing? The police are here now."

He whirls at me. OH, SO NOW YOU'LL TALK TO ME. NOW IT'S DIF-FERENT, IS IT?

"Lloyd, you don't have to do this, please don't do this."

I'VE GOT PROOF, YOONA. HE'S ALIVE. YOU CAN'T GO THROUGH WITH IT NOW. ADMIT IT.

He means you, and my heart drops every time I'm reminded that you're dead.

"I don't understand," Daiyu whimpers. "What's happening?"

I can't explain. I don't even know myself how Lloyd turned into this. Or is it I who turned into someone who could make him do this?

"What proof do you have?" I say.

I WON'T LET YOU LIE ANYMORE. I LOVED YOU.

Don't listen to him. It's not what you imagine love is. I never chose him over you. Don't think I forgot about you. I didn't. He doesn't mean that kind of love, the one you and I had. He means something else. Something he imagined into being.

"Lloyd, you've got to accept it's over," I repeat. He acts as if he doesn't hear me and points the shotgun at Daiyu. I hold my breath. And then he lowers the gun and takes a thick roll of gray duct tape out of his coat pocket. He waves it in Heather's direction. AROUND HER WRISTS AND FEET. DO IT NOW.

When he throws the tape at Daiyu, she misses it. It hits the floor and rolls, and I bend to retrieve it.

He lunges at me, snatches the tape out of my hands, and shoves it into Daiyu's. DO IT. NOW. He backs away, raising the shotgun at Daiyu's head. Tears pour down her cheeks as Heather holds out her arms

6

and says, "Do what he wants. It's okay, it's just for now, it'll be okay, Daiyu." I meet Heather's eyes, and she looks over at Faye, and I see that Faye has moved toward the door. Lloyd is intent on Daiyu, watching her fumble, her fingers pulling the end of the tape. Faye maneuvers a little closer to the door.

"I'll listen to you, whatever it is. Let the girls go and we'll talk. Put the gun away. If you have proof, show me, and we'll explain to the police," I tell him.

He looks at me with hate, and I flinch. Without looking at Faye, he steps sideways and nabs Faye's ponytailed hair. WHERE ARE YOU GOING?

10

I read a statistic that women who were abused as children have a higher likelihood of being in abusive adult relationships. Physical, sexual, all of it. This didn't make sense to me. I thought it would be the opposite. I thought it was like what Willa's friend Albert said about his sister, how she'd been raped and so she never sat on a couch with other people after that. She always chose a chair. A single chair, where no one could sit next to her. After the rape, she couldn't stand to have a man close to her. Which was why, he said, she wasn't married now and probably wouldn't ever be in a relationship again. I thought about that. Did this apply to those who witnessed abuse too?

11

Daiyu has finished taping Heather's and Faye's wrists. They're sitting on the edge of my bed. She's working on Heather's ankles. Lloyd has barricaded the door with my desk and chair. "You don't mean to do this, Lloyd. Think about it for a second. This isn't going to help Jaesung or you. How can you help Jaesung when you're in jail?"

You shut up. He grabs the tape from Daiyu and throws it at me. I catch it, an instinct to keep it from hitting me in the face. It's a fat new reel, and it stings my hands. I put it on the desk. If I push it aside and then move the chair, I can open the door and escape. Except he will shoot me in the back. Except my friends will be left with him.

I said your ankles.

I pick up the tape and loosen the end. It smells like plastic and gasoline.

"I'm not going anywhere, Lloyd," I tell him.

If I didn't bring Daiyu here, you would never have let me in. Tape your fucking feet or—

He takes a handgun out of his other pocket. What else does he have in that long wool coat? The handgun is a black square-nosed thing. He pushes the muzzle into Daiyu's head.

"Yoona," she whimpers.

I sit beside Faye and Heather. I tape my ankles together, but not completely, only the front where he can see. He sends Daiyu over to wrap my wrists. The sound of sirens is all around us. Still coming and fading, and now not fading anymore. With so many police cars outside, in a few minutes we'll be free, won't we? All I have to do is buy us some time. I hold out my wrists to Daiyu, who has not stopped crying. The tears will keep the tape from sticking, I think, and move my hands so her tears land on the sticky part of the tape, but she doesn't understand and presses the tape down. I shake my head. "I'm so sorry, Yoona," she sobs.

You're joining them. Lloyd pushes Daiyu next to me. In one swish he has bound Daiyu's hands, and he hauls her to her feet and puts her on the other side of Heather. He hasn't taped her ankles. My heart lingers on that small fact. The way she curls up, he won't notice. Will that help us out of this situation somehow?

8

Then he returns to my side. And my heart sinks. We're all in a row. Ducks in a row. And he's too close. I can smell his sweat like rancid milk. He holds the handgun up in front of my face. TAKE A GOOD LOOK AT IT. YOU COULD HAVE BEEN WITH ME, ON THIS SIDE, THE WAY WE PLANNED. YOU'RE MAKING ME DO THIS. ALL YOUR LIES. I GAVE YOU A CHANCE.

The sirens suddenly stop. He runs to the window overlooking the parking lot, slams the window closed, yanks the left and then the right panel of the curtains. They're the dark-blue blackout sort. Weston splurged this year. Suddenly it's dark except for a sliver of light that Lloyd allows by pulling back an edge with a finger so he can see the parking lot. It's quieter now in the room. I can make out the muffled sound of car doors slamming and low voices speaking. Someone whistles as if signaling to someone else. Gravel crunches underfoot. More cars drive up, and engines are cut off.

The phone rings, and Lloyd snatches the receiver and holds it up to his ear but doesn't let it touch his head, as if he thinks the police can send poisonous gas through it.

THEY'RE FINE. UNLESS YOU DO SOMETHING STUPID. UNDERSTAND? He thrusts the phone at me. TELL HIM I HAVEN'T HURT ANYONE.

I speak into the mouthpiece. "He hasn't, but hurry." Daiyu and Faye join in with their own "Hurry." Lloyd snatches the phone away, and I can feel his breath on my cheek as he holds the phone between us. SHUT UP OR ELSE I'LL FUCKING TAPE YOUR MOUTHS TOO. They stop.

A man's voice is on the other end of the phone. He says his name is Detective Sax, he asks if we're okay, and I look to Lloyd, who nods, so I tell him we're four of us, four girls. "It's going to be okay, I promise," Sax says with such composure I think I might be dreaming this whole thing. "How many gunmen, did you say?" he asks.

"One."

"Try to stay calm, we're working on getting you out of there, I promise. If he has a list of demands, tell him to write them down, and I'll try to get them for him, relax," he continues.

"His name is Lloyd, Lloyd Kang," I reply, and Lloyd removes the phone and slams it into its cradle. I DIDN'T TELL YOU TO TELL HIM MY NAME, he howls and holds the butt of the shotgun above my head.

Daiyu and Faye gasp.

"Don't, Lloyd. If you hurt us, you won't get anything you want," I tell him, looking up at him.

He stares at me, and I can see his eyes are rimmed in red as if he's rubbed them too hard. YOU DON'T EVEN CARE IF HE DIES IN A NORTH KOREAN SHITHOLE.

"But he's not alive, Lloyd," I remind him. I can't make myself call you dead. "The accident in Korea, you remember, he's gone. There's no one to save."

YOU LIE, he spits, lowering the shotgun. Where's the handgun? Is it close to me on the bed? YOU DON'T EVEN LOVE HIM. I CAN PROVE HE'S ALIVE. WHAT ARE YOU GOING TO DO THEN? HOW ARE YOU GOING TO EXPLAIN TO HIM WHAT YOU WERE GOING TO DO UNTIL I STOPPED YOU?

He waves the shotgun at all of us. YOU'RE GOING TO FREE HIM. HE'S WORTH A HUNDRED OF YOU.

12

Once, in my high school gym, I stepped off the bleachers from the top row, expecting to make my way down as everyone else was doing at the end of a school rally. As soon as my foot found air, I knew something was wrong. Instead of finding a foothold on the level below me, I was falling, and I told myself, *I'm falling: I must have time because I'm aware of this, and here is air around me, space and air, I'm falling, I can move my arms, I can put out my hands and brace my fall.* So move, now, I told myself, move your arms, get your hands ready. My mind told my hands, my arms, even my legs to adjust, and I was convinced I could still make this happen even as my shoulder slammed onto the polished wooden basketball court, even as my head followed suit, making contact with the surface—I believed I had a chance to affect the way I landed. Stunned, I couldn't believe how fast the floor had risen to greet me. Hard, unforgivingly hard, and my body ached. I lifted my head. What had happened to my chance? My sister looked down at me from the fifth row, where I'd been moments before, and said, "You fell like a rock."

13

We sit and wait. Why isn't Detective Sax calling again? Faye leans into me, and I lean into her. Heather, on the other side of Faye, sits up tall. Daiyu leans into Heather. Lloyd paces, twitching and mumbling at something on his shoulder. From outside, in the direction of the parking lot, come sounds of car doors slamming shut and tires crunching gravel. Loud voices call to each other. I HAVE PROOF. I HAVE PROOF, Lloyd mutters as he paces. He jerks the gun around his body. He and the shotgun are one unit, and we are stuck in our places. I hold my breath. He levels the gun with his other hand, pointing it at each of us one by one. I'LL KILL THEM. I WILL. YOU KNOW I CAN, he shouts at the ceiling.

It's Heather who talks to him. "The police aren't going to let you just kill us. They'll come in any minute. Give up right now and save yourself."

14

It's my fault my friends are in this room facing this crazy man. Heather's room is two doors down from mine. I met Heather on the day I moved in. Her little brother ran into me with a stuffed toy Dalmatian in his hands. Later Heather introduced me to Faye, who was her roommate. Daiyu was in Faye's biology lab. Clear line, friend to friend to friend.

15

My hands are tingling. The tape is too tight around my wrists. I have to get out of this somehow. What can I say to Lloyd to make him let us go? What would you say if you were here? You would say we had to try, no matter what, that we could never give up.

The phone rings, and Lloyd holds it up in the air. Sax's voice comes through. "You sound like a reasonable person, Lloyd. We can work this out. We don't want this to get out of hand. I'm here to help you."

YOU'RE THE BALD MAN IN THE LONG COAT, AREN'T YOU?

"I want to help you."

I'VE GOT THE SAME COAT. WHAT ABOUT THAT?

"That's a good start, Lloyd. How can I help you?"

My heart catches in my throat. Will it be as easy as that? Sax will give Lloyd what he wants. Lloyd is sweating and keeps wiping his face with the palms of his hands, which have dirt and grime on them. Each time he wipes his face he leaves streaks of black and brown on it. The phone doesn't reach the window overlooking the parking lot, so Lloyd runs back and forth to see what's going on outside as he talks to Sax on the phone.

"I WANT PRESIDENT REAGAN, PRESIDENT CHUN DOO HWAN, AND KIM IL SUNG TO MEET WITH ME PRIVATELY."

"Now we're getting somewhere," Sax says without missing a beat. Is it every day that someone requests a meeting with three world leaders? Hope rises in me again. We can hear Detective Sax's voice on the phone because it's quiet otherwise, so quiet otherwise, as if everyone outside has frozen in place too and is listening intently, even the birds. Lloyd holds the phone away from his ear, out to us.

Sax is talking. "I understand. Give me some time. You're talking about the White House."

YES. THE WHITE FUCKING HOUSE. I'LL TRADE THESE GIRLS FOR JAESUNG KIM. HE'S AN AMERICAN STUDENT IN NORTH KOREA RIGHT THIS MINUTE. LET HIM GO, OR ELSE THESE GIRLS AREN'T GOING TO MAKE IT THROUGH THIS. DON'T THINK I WON'T DO IT. REAGAN, CHUN DOO HWAN, KIM IL SUNG. IN THAT ORDER.

"You mean the leaders of North Korea and South Korea and President Reagan?"

My heart falters. Sax doesn't sound as confident as he did a moment ago.

Lloyd's voice rises. ARE YOU STUPID, OR ARE THESE GIRLS NOT WORTH IT? IS THAT WHAT YOU'RE SAYING? YOU GOING TO TELL THEIR PARENTS THAT?

"It's the other side of the world, that's all, Lloyd. What else? Can I get you something else? Work with me, Lloyd."

THE FUTURE OF THE WORLD DEPENDS ON FREEING JAESUNG KIM.

"Tell me about Jaesung Kim."

YOU THINK I'M STUPID? YOU'RE STALLING. GET ME WHAT I WANT. I'VE GOT FOUR GIRLS IN HERE. I'LL SHOOT THEM. DON'T THINK I WON'T.

"Listen, I'm just making sure. We have to be sure. I wouldn't want to get the wrong president."

FUCKING ASSHOLE, PATRONIZING ASSHOLE.

"Wait, wait, listen, I said it wrong. Let's be realistic: getting the president—you're talking leaders of three countries—will take some time. Let me help you. You need any food? Water, anything at all until we can arrange what you want?"

YOU'RE STALLING AGAIN.

"I'm being helpful. Let me help you, Lloyd. But let me be clear, you won't get to talk to the president if you hurt anyone. I work with you; you work with me. Agreed?"

DON'T BULLSHIT ME. YOU'VE GOT ONE HOUR.

Lloyd slams the phone down into its cradle.

16

The first weekend after classes started, Heather and I went to a party in the student union. I could hear music pounding from the room, Prince's "Purple Rain," as we approached a large gothic building in the arts quadrangle. All paths converged there, and everyone walked in crowds toward that building. It was dark by eight, but there were so many lights on around the quad and the student union that it seemed like daytime. Huge spotlights were set up on the grass outside, and tables with signs inviting students to join this athletic club or that community service group were everywhere.

That night could have been a new start, as it was for many freshmen like me. Everyone was friendly and open, easy to talk to, smiling. The air was festive. In Korea, the last time I had seen you, you'd said to me, "Freshmen have to suffer," and sent me away. I found myself making note of things to tell you when I saw you again. The stone staircase up to a large terrace outside the entrance with more tables covered with flyers announcing clubs for political organizations and campus newspapers. Apparently there were two rival publications, one that was radical and one that toed the official college line. The conversations about President Reagan and the economy, the talk of South Africa's apartheid system and how other colleges were protesting. *You would feel at home here,* I thought, as I signed my name to the mailing list for the radical newspaper.

Heather waved to a group of students by the door when we entered the building, and we walked over to them. One of them had gone to her high school. I tried to pay attention when introductions were made.

I met Daiyu and Faye that night. Daiyu lived in Taft, the modern concrete-block behemoth across the quadrangle of buildings of the main campus. Uglier on the outside than Reynolds, where Heather, Faye, and I had our rooms, Taft was reputed to have plush new mauve carpeting and had more bathrooms per floor than our dorm. All freshmen were housed in these two buildings. The four of us walked around, picking up flyers, signing up for clubs. Faye laughed about everything, and Heather and I looked at each other wondering why. "I'm sorry, I have this problem," Faye said. "I get silly spells." Then she burst into laughter again and tried to stop it, resulting in loud hiccups. I wondered if she was on drugs. Or was it immaturity? Silly spells? Didn't we use words like that in third grade? Daiyu tripped three times on our walk to the dorms. She was the accident-prone one.

I tried to relax around them, my new friends. There was nothing to hide, unlike the way it had been back in high school. I had nothing to hide, because my parents were in Lakeburg. And you had done something to me; meeting you had changed me. I felt it. I could stop and look around and take in the looks of others without feeling embarrassed or ashamed. I could weather being inspected for once and not squirm under their gaze. "Let them look," you used to say. "Let them. Be yourself."

17

What would Willa do in my place here in this room?

My sister, Willa, was always falling in love. I don't know how she could when our parents were poor examples of what follows after you fall in love. The old childhood limerick that Willa welcomed—Willa and Tom or Eric or whoever she had a crush on that week sitting in a tree, K-I-S-S-I-N-G, first comes love, then comes marriage, then comes baby in a baby carriage. But you know, for me, love was something I resisted. Even with you.

My sister was the social one at school. She had loads of friends and spent her time after school and on weekends at her friends' houses. Boyfriends kept her out of the house when she got older. She avoided all things Korean as if they were the reason our father lost his temper. How could I blame her? Being Korean seemed to be the reason for his rage.

"They make fun of my English," he used to shout as he threw a chair to the floor. "I don't get the promotion, I don't get the raise. What are you looking at?"

It seemed all I could do was hold up the test I'd taken at school as he made his way toward my mother. "See my A-plus," I said to him. "Look, look."

Sometimes it worked, his eyes registered what was on the page; sometimes it was as if I were invisible. "How are we going to protect our children from this?" he shouted before he knocked our dinner off the table. I said, "I'm here, right here. Stop, stop, stop." But he ignored me. I ran from him to my mother, back and forth, waving my hands. Look at me, stop, stop, stop.

18

I've read that the five stages of grief are denial and isolation, anger, bargaining, depression, and acceptance. Is it denial if I speak to you in my head as if you're alive somewhere and can hear me?

19

Two months before I started at Weston College in central Pennsylvania, I went to Korea. It was July 6, 1985. I boarded a plane at the county airport near Lakeburg, New York, transferred at Kennedy Airport in New York City three hours later, and flew to the other side of the world. You and I were on the same plane that left New York City, along with several others who had just graduated from high school or had done so the year before. You were one of those who had graduated from high school a year earlier and had already finished one year of college. I didn't see you on the plane, which is hard to believe now. How did I not notice you?

The first time I saw you was in Gimpo Airport in Seoul after we landed. I was in the crowd behind you, making my way to the exits. You and another boy, who could have been your brother except for the widow's peak that made your hair jut out over your forehead, were shaking hands with men and women on the other side of the cordoned-off hallway, perfectly at ease. Men in business suits or patterned button-down shirts open at the neck to show white T-shirts underneath reached across and patted you on the back. Women in knee-length floral dresses in muted colors with their hair styled and pressed powder on their cheeks waved you in closer to see if you were who they sought. Everyone there looked more formal than those of us who had arrived from the States in our bright, casual vacation clothes.

You smiled and leaned in with a stranger's hand still in yours to hear what he or she said. You blushed at the compliments. There must have been compliments. You had a glow about you, a confidence. And you charmed those hundreds of people reaching to touch us as we walked off the plane, reaching for our clothes, our hands, our elbows, as if touching us would make us become who they wanted us to be—their loved one, relative, or dongchang, old childhood friend.

It was my first international flight, and on the other side of the world I shrank from those throngs even as I saw you and your friend

17

reach out to them, and I thought how arrogant you were. And I also thought how kind, even as I hurried past. I didn't think I'd see either one of you again.

I had immigrated to the United States when I was a year old, and here I was seventeen years later. I remembered nothing from back then, of course. The entire experience was new. My uncle, my mother's sister's husband, was a legal adviser in the government, so I was immediately swept away by his chauffeur. You expected it to be so. "You have a princess telephone in your bedroom," you said to me later. And I couldn't admit you were right about that. I had a white-and-gold phone on my white-and-gold dresser in my gold-wallpapered bedroom in Lakeburg, New York. But the rest of what happened in my house was a secret I didn't tell you.

Outside the airport, the air was heavy with July monsoon-season rain, and my uncle's small black Daewoo sedan was conveniently waiting for me curbside along with dozens of other cars lined up, occupied and not, with people shouting and whistles of traffic officers shrieking. The chauffeur referred to the other teenagers and me that day as jemi kyopo. "Korean students who study abroad," he explained in Korean.

"But I'm American," I said in my hesitant Korean.

"Doesn't matter," he replied.

20

No matter what Lloyd says here now in this room, don't believe the part that he loved me. That I gave him the impression that I loved him. You're the only one I ever loved. I don't know what he means by you being alive or how he can save you by killing us. I wanted to believe Lloyd at first. I wanted to believe you had survived as he had survived. I wish I could believe him now, but he's ranting like a lunatic, and he has guns. And I've pushed him to this—it's my fault he's enraged. But I couldn't help it. I wanted him to be right about you.

21

I remember in Korea, driving from the airport that day, I saw a girl on a corner, no more than a child herself, with a sleeping baby tied to her back, kneeling on the concrete. At another intersection, a man my father's age with a blue cap on was riding a green bicycle. He cut in front of us and then swerved just as suddenly out of sight in the sea of glinting cars ahead. A man with a bent back pulling a wooden-wheeled cart, too old to be doing such work, came into view. I saw an old woman in a white hanbok, her silver hair in a neat roll at the nape of her neck, a white handkerchief in her hand, held to her mouth. She was coughing. Standing still in the middle of the street, nearly motionless in front of an uneven row of small Hyundai and Daewoo sedans all edging forward. For a moment I thought she'd be struck by one of them. I leaned forward. Her eyes looked straight into mine as our car passed. She leaned toward us, and our car brushed her chima. Or was it just our speed that made her skirt billow for an instant? Wait.

At one of the stoplights, a woman my mother's age, an ajumma, my mother would have said, an auntie, stood by the curb. With a gap in her front teeth, her gums receded to the point that I could see the beginning of her teeth's roots, where the white narrowed. She tapped my window. I unrolled it.

"Let me touch your face," I heard her say in Korean.

I recoiled in my seat behind the driver.

"Not 'touch,'" the chauffeur said to me as if reading my mind. "Turn closer to her. She wants to see your face."

I did as he directed. The woman spoke again, but I didn't understand her words this time, and the driver shook his head. "I see the resemblance," he answered.

"What does she mean?" I asked him.

The woman's hand, calloused, stroked mine on the sill of the car door.

"She thinks you look like Yuk Yeong Su, President Park's wife. Park was president before President Chun. You have the same complexion, white like powder. She was a beauty. Too bad about her death." Then he said to the woman, "My dear, we must go. Careful now," in such a gentle voice I thought they must secretly rendezvous at this light every day.

When the car lurched forward, my stomach jumped to the back of the seat. I swallowed. We cruised easily down the street, one of a million of those tiny cars, to my aunt's apartment in Seoul. She had two maids: one who lived in the apartment with her and another who came every day to help out. They cooked and cleaned. I thought my aunt treated them well. She said everyone had at least one person who worked for them. "It's not like America," she said.

She had two children, both a handful of years older than I was, both married. She insisted I take a short nap before we went out for lunch. I was surprised at how quickly I fell asleep. She had laid out a bed for me on the floor, a yo, a thick futon with layers of blankets on it and then a thin cotton comforter to pull up over myself. The rest of the hardwood bedroom floor was covered in a large green bamboo mat that felt cool to my feet. The smell of bamboo after the smoke and exhaust from city streets was calming. I fell asleep imagining I was lying in a cool wooded hollow.

22

I used to climb out of my window to sit on my roof and watch the car lights go up and down the avenue. Where were they going? Inside my house came sounds of furniture being overturned. I'd tried once to stop my father's rage by calling the police, but when the patrol cars pulled into our driveway, the furniture was right side up again and the door was opened to reveal a pleasant set of parents. Upstanding citizens. They explained it was a misunderstanding. A wayward child. A child on punishment who was playing a prank. I watched the whole encounter from the landing of the staircase. The police officers didn't call me down to question me. My father offered them tea, and my mother went to the kitchen to prepare it. He was careful never to strike her on the face.

I went back upstairs, clambered out through my bedroom window, and huddled on the roof under the branch of the oak tree. I could picture it: the fall forward on the sloping roof of my old house and the feel of the sparkly shingles on my head and back and arms as I rolled down, hit the gutter and the yard. Not high enough to be fatal, but it made me think I should stop fighting.

23

The phone rings. Lloyd grabs it and is at attention, listening to every word, the handset pressed against his ear. Is President Reagan on the phone right now? Then he thrusts the receiver at me. TELL HIM I HAVEN'T HURT ANY OF YOU.

Faye, Heather, and Daiyu hold their breaths. Heather's cheek has stopped bleeding.

"Lloyd?" I can hear Sax's voice, and he sounds friendly.

"He hasn't done anything to us," I reply.

"He's not forcing you to lie, is he?" Sax's voice is tentative.

Lloyd presses his head closer, which rams the phone against my ear, which makes me call out in surprise and pain, and Sax says, "What's going on?"

"No," I say louder than I mean to. "He's not making me say anything. We're fine."

Lloyd pats my back, the gun in his hand. GOOD.

Sax says, "What sorts of weapons does he have?"

FUCKING TELL HIM I WANT THE PRESIDENT. I'VE DONE MY PART—NOW MAKE HIM DO HIS. DAMN IT.

"A lot. He has a lot. Please let him talk to the president."

"What's your name, honey?"

"My name?"

Lloyd takes the phone away from me. WHY DOES THAT MATTER? WHERE'S REAGAN?

Heather, Faye, and Daiyu call out their names toward the phone. Lloyd pushes me toward Faye, and we topple like dominoes. It would make anyone laugh until they saw our bound hands and feet and the desperation in our eyes.

WHAT'S THE PROBLEM? YOU DON'T BELIEVE ME?

"We do, we do, Lloyd." Sax's voice comes through. He's speaking in a loud voice. A firm, loud voice that comes through the handset into this room that is blisteringly quiet otherwise. "Calm down. I've been on the job for twenty years, and I've never lost one of these. We'll help you, I promise."

I'LL ONLY TALK TO THE PRESIDENT ABOUT IT. EVERYONE IS IN ON IT. EVEN YOU. THE WHOLE POLICE DEPARTMENT, THE CIA. EVERYONE. I WILL ONLY TALK TO PRESIDENT REAGAN.

"And don't forget the leaders of North and South Korea."

YES.

"I'm paying attention, Lloyd. Don't you worry about it. But listen, the flight alone from DC is going to take several hours to arrange."

YOU'RE A LIAR. BESIDES AIR FORCE ONE FLIES AT SUPERSONIC SPEED.

"That's not quite true, Lloyd. What about a phone call with the president? Will that help your friend Jaesung Kim?"

IN PERSON. DO IT. GET HIM HERE. I CAN SHOW HIM JAESUNG KIM IS ALIVE.

"And the leaders of North and South Korea will arrive tomorrow. How's that? Once we get you out of there, we can put you up in a hotel, and you can wait for them comfortably. Arrange a nice visit, a real high-level meeting."

I TOLD YOU AN HOUR—NOW IT'S FORTY-FIVE MINUTES OR ELSE THE FIRST GIRL DIES.

24

After eight days with my aunt in Seoul, I was ready for the student tour. I settled in my seat on one of three buses with my headphones on. Several of us sat by ourselves, while many more sat together talking as if they already knew each other. I was used to it, not having many friends back home. I didn't expect to make friends here. The doors of the bus were nearly closed when they abruptly reversed, and the two boys I'd seen in the airport bounded on board. We all looked up and watched them make their way down the aisle. I was seated in the middle row of the bus, on the right-hand side, by a window. I returned to listening to music. It was a cassette of songs by Yong Pil Cho that I'd bought while shopping with my aunt.

I looked out the window. I remember how hot it was that day, hot enough for the humidity to cloud the streets, and here we were on an overly cooled bus. I pulled my sweater over my bare legs to warm up. Like all the students from the States, I was wearing shorts. So I wasn't paying attention when these boys who got on the bus late asked for something. And then they were in my row, and I heard the tour guide up front tell them just to sit down, anywhere, the bus had to depart.

One of the boys said, "All right, all right," and took an aisle seat across from me. But the other one kept asking, his hand on the seat back beside mine, and I noticed his pinkie was missing its upper half, no knuckle or nail portion above the first knuckle. I looked to see if it was folded over, but when he moved his hand, I could see clearly that it was shortened.

No one was willing to give up a window seat. "Just sit," the boy who had taken a seat said to the one standing. "We'll be across from each other."

I pulled my headphones off and picked up my sweater and my book. "I'll switch," I told him.

The boy in the seat across the aisle said, "Thanks, but it's fine." That was Lloyd. But you, you were the other boy, and you gave me the most grateful smile. "Would you really?" you said. I slid out of my row, and you made room for me and then told Lloyd to take the window seat where I'd been seconds ago.

"You were on the plane. I remember you," you said, leaning over the aisle after you settled into your seat next to Lloyd. I was about to put my headphones back on. Instead I said, "What happened to your finger?"

You held up your left hand. "You mean this?" you said, then lowered it again. "I was born with it."

"Sorry, it's none of my business." I felt my face flush from embarrassment.

"Usually takes people a while to ask."

"Maybe they think it but don't ask," I said.

"I don't care what other people think. What are you listening to?" you asked, looking at my Walkman.

I showed you the cassette cover, and you told me you hadn't heard Cho or much Korean music. The relatives you were staying with had shared Swedish music they liked. We leaned across the aisle between us. I didn't want it to stop. You translated the lyrics for me; your Korean was better than mine. You'd asked your father to teach you how to read, and from there you'd read whatever you could get your hands on, though most of your parents' Korean books had been decades old.

You said things I'd never put into words but had felt myself—about wishing for context, wanting some idea of who we were and if it even mattered. That was the same day I told you about the chauffeur's comparison of my face to President Park's wife's.

You shuddered at the mention of President Park. "Admired for being a dictator. I don't get it," you said.

"The chauffeur was talking about his wife. Said she was beautiful and I looked like her."

"He was hitting on you."

"No way. There was a woman on the street who—"

"Yeah, figures."

"No, it was about her skin—no one said I was beautiful in Lakeburg, and—"

"Definitely hitting on you. Did he ask you out?"

"No, he's way older. He works for my aunt."

"So?"

"That's weird."

"You're weirder."

"Thanks a lot."

You laughed, and I had to join you. You had that effect on me. I couldn't help it. You made me feel as if everything could be all right.

We talked nonstop the whole ride out of Seoul about wanting to know more about Korea. I was surprised at how comfortable I was talking to you. We were alike. You were eager to soak it all up. Being born in the States, in North Dakota, had made you feel isolated. We leaned across the aisle and talked as if no one else existed on that bus. I'd never talked as easily before with anyone. And you asked questions about the future. "What do you want to do, Yoona? With your life, I mean. Isn't it crazy we have to know right now? But do you? Do you know?" And

25

I agreed, the future loomed. No one else seemed as aware of it, but I was worried. I couldn't imagine myself any older than I was. I didn't want to be, and you said you understood that. You couldn't see it either and wondered how others did, how others were clear about what the future had in store for them. You must have known somehow that you wouldn't be around to see what happened.

25

We've righted ourselves now and huddle together on the edge of the bed. Lloyd has returned to the window, looking out and muttering to himself. There's no way President Reagan is meeting with a stranger with a gun. A chill even colder than I thought possible seeps deeper into my chest. He said he'd kill one of us. Faye says over and over again, "Oh my god, oh my god." Heather whispers, "Shh . . . it'd be stupid, he needs us alive."

Daiyu whispers back, "There's four of us, Heather. He doesn't need all four of us."

"Stop, he'll hear you," I say to them, but he has heard already, and he bounds over to us. I DECIDE. ME. I DECIDE WHO LIVES AND DIES. YOU GET IT?

He can't mean it, he can't mean he'll do it, but I would never have believed we'd be here like this if you'd told me. You would know how to persuade him.

He hauls Daiyu to her feet. "No, no, no, no," she squeals. COME ON. He pulls. I wonder if I can move my feet just enough to make it to the door. Watching her head hanging in front, I feel pity and then have a burst of hope for her. *Run, Daiyu,* I urge silently. As if I've said it aloud, she looks back, and there's nothing but fear in her eyes. I realize that she thinks he's going to shoot her, thinks that he meant her when

26

he said the first girl would die. WHAT ARE YOU LOOKING AT? He jerks her arm so she turns around, faces the window. "Don't kill me, please," she says.

Run, Daiyu, I think. *Pull away. Hit him with your bound fists and run for the door, push away the desk and the chair. If you're fast, Daiyu, he won't have a chance to shoot you.* "Daiyu!" I call to her.

SHUT UP. Lloyd shoves her in front of the window.

Lloyd sweeps one half of the curtain aside with an arm, avoids standing in front of it himself. The sunlight is shocking. Like on an airplane when you're flying in the dark and dawn arrives through someone's window. I raise my wrists to keep the light from hurting my eyes. Heather and Faye turn their faces. He holds Daiyu in front of the window but stays off to the side himself. Daiyu flinches from the light and whatever is on the other side. Line of fire. "Duck down," I yell to her. She bends, and he jerks her back up. He could break her arm, snap it, she protests. She says he's hurting her. Her shoulders are shaking. He tells her to hold up her hands so they can see he's taped them. He holds the handgun against her temple.

"Someone's in the hall, Lloyd, don't." Words like this tumble from my mouth, and I hardly know I have the breath to speak.

FUCK. He throws Daiyu to the floor and slams the curtain closed, then runs to the side of the door. It's dark again in the room. BACK UP, FUCKING BACK UP, OR I'LL KILL ALL OF THEM RIGHT NOW.

26

You and Lloyd used to go running when the rest of us were laid out under the giant fans in the Great Hall, massed together the way we were in Korea that summer. Lazy American teenagers who didn't know how to cope with tropical weather, the humidity cloaking our bodies. I saw

Lloyd. I saw the way he replied to your questions about political factions in the Korean government, about North Korea's leader Kim Il Sung. I saw him wave his hands and explain. You told me something about Lloyd, about his childhood, but I didn't pay attention. I wanted to know about you, only you. I miss you, I miss you, I miss you. What have I done?

27

I didn't believe my father when he told me his version of love. "You kill for it sometimes," he said. "I would kill for your mother, you, and your sister. I've seen people kill for less."

We were driving in the car, and he pointed to a smokestack in a city like Bethlehem, Pennsylvania, and he said, "Yoona, tell me, what does that smoke coming up over there tell you about the direction of the wind?" I was six years old. Willa made a face at him. "No fair, you asked me that two years ago, and Yoona heard your answer."

"I don't remember what you said," I told her.

"Stupid," Willa said.

"You're stupid," I returned.

"I see a rest stop," my mother interrupted. "Who needs to use the bathroom?" She told my father to pull over, and when he did, my mother insisted Willa get out of the car with her while my father and I waited for them. He turned on the radio, which was a relief because he never said anything to me when my mother and sister weren't around anyway, and I didn't have to answer his question about smoke. The announcer said someone had murdered someone with a knife over an insult in a parking lot. "That's stupid," I said aloud. That's when my father said Americans have no patience and then added Koreans know about suffering. Long-term suffering. "You have to be patient. You have to endure for people you love. I'd kill to protect your mother, your sister, and you. That's what war shows you. You kill to survive. To survive, you'd eat a handful of uncooked rice, even." I didn't ask him where his patience was when he lost his temper in our house. I knew better. He was the kind of person who believed his own lies. Other people confused me, but not him. Many people confused me. My mother, for example. Why did she stay with my father?

28

I didn't know how much you'd understand about my family. And I couldn't tell you, not when you thought I was like you. You would never have let your father beat your mother. You would have thrown yourself between them. I never did that. Why didn't I do that? Instead I pleaded from a distance. Many times I was too late. Just before I got on the plane to Korea, I came home to find my mother in the kitchen, her hand on a drawer handle by the stove and my father standing over her. He walked off when I entered, and I helped my mother to her feet, and we gathered her coat and car keys, and I drove her down the driveway and away from him forever. I told her it was forever, and she agreed she'd never return to the house. And then as we neared the town limits, she said she had to go back. She'd left soup on the stove, and she had to go back to turn off the heat. I ignored her, driving on, but she insisted. At a stop light she even opened the door, and I turned the car around, telling myself it was only for the soup. But I knew I'd failed to save her.

29

"Someone's in the hall, Lloyd," I repeat. Watching Lloyd by the door listening to see if I'm right shows me I could have a plan. I can convince him of whatever I want. Heather must understand, because she says, "I heard it too."

Lloyd kicks the door. GET ME THE PRESIDENT, DAMN IT. GET OUT OF HERE. I'LL SHOW YOU I MEAN IT.

There's silence on the other side.

In another minute, he'll start shooting through the door. I start talking. "You showed them you aren't stupid. And you showed them Daiyu— you've done your part," I tell him.

He whirls toward me. I'LL SHOW THEM A DEAD GIRL. THAT'LL PUT PRESIDENTS ON A PLANE.

The phone rings, and Lloyd lunges for it. But this time he crouches down, huddling on the floor by me as if he thinks they'll storm in and the bed will shield him. Daiyu remains underneath the window, a whimpering lump. Heather and Faye are as still as statues.

WHAT GAME ARE YOU PLAYING? Lloyd shouts into the phone.

"No games, Lloyd. I'm trying to reach the president, just like you asked. He's a busy man. It takes time to work these things out. What were you doing at the window with that girl?"

GET YOUR MEN OUT OF THE HALL.

"No one's in the building, Lloyd. It's been evacuated. That's the protocol. We get you your demands, and you free the girls, and everyone goes home safely."

I'M DOING THIS TO STOP WORLD WAR THREE. TELL THE PRESIDENT THAT.

"While we're waiting for the president, why don't you tell me if there's anything else you want? Maybe we can arrange for you to go to DC instead of him coming to you."

THAT'S BULLSHIT.

"I've been straight with you, Lloyd. I'm just a local cop trying to reach the president of the United States for you. Let me help you while we wait."

I TOLD YOU AN HOUR. IT'S BEEN THIRTY MINUTES. IF ANYONE COMES THROUGH THAT DOOR, I'LL START SHOOTING. ALL IN A ROW. ALL IN FRONT OF ME. DON'T MAKE ME DO IT.

His voice is rising, and any minute now he'll do it, he'll kill all of us. Could we pile on top of him, kick the gun away? He's close enough to me for me to pound him with my hands tied together like a hammer. I look to Heather, and she nods. But then Lloyd lurches up suddenly and grabs Heather, yanks her, and she falls sideways, hard, to the floor. She cries out.

30

My first instinct when I met Lloyd on the bus in Korea was to be wary. I didn't know why. You didn't suspect anything, or maybe you already knew and understood him better than I did. You might have seen the signs from Lloyd that this was coming. You tried to tell me things. The student tour took us around the country in a caravan of buses, with flags waving. We were escorted by government vehicles, cars, and motorcycles. We went through red lights. Cars, buses, and other police vehicles stopped for us. They saluted us. Us. Americans touring Korea. We looked out the windows and complained that the air-conditioning wasn't on high enough in our luxury buses with their plush, clean upholstered seats and scented restroom (even if it was an awful, flowery scent), weaving through the streets of Seoul. We, the privileged young people from abroad, spoiled with the conveniences of modern life in America. You and I rolled our eyes at the entitlement we heard throughout the bus. You and I knew better, and I guess Lloyd did too, but he was angrier about it. He slammed the heel of his hand onto the back of our seats when he pointed out the injustices. I saw this early on, the peripheries of his rage.

You were tender in contrast. I never saw you rage out of control about anything. Like the tip of your shortened finger, your fury was born missing. And you were always giving money away, even though I found out eventually you hardly had any yourself. Your parents were professors at a community college in North Dakota, and their salaries were not high. You said you wished you liked biology so you could share your father's passion with him, but you leaned more toward your mother's expertise in ancient history.

We were taken to the Seokguram Buddha on one of the first afternoons on the Korea tour. After that first conversation on the bus, it had been harder to be alone with you. Lloyd and others were always there talking to you about what was in the news. They pointed out political demonstrations that were taking place throughout Korea. Remember Jerry with the Yankees cap who sat behind you and the girl from Michigan who disagreed with both of you about the aim of the protesters? I listened and asked questions, but they drowned me out. When we arrived at the Seokguram Buddha, I decided to explore by myself, and to be honest, I didn't trust this sudden onset of whatever I was feeling toward you. It felt like the beginning of obsession or addiction or love.

I went ahead with the crowd and left you and Lloyd and Jerry to debate the merits of one political party over the other. When I saw it, I stopped in my tracks. Before me was a gigantic solid-gold Buddha, sitting on a lotus pedestal. A dozen feet tall on a pedestal half his size, he sat cross-legged in his classic pose, palms open, back of his hands resting on his knees. The massive, serene face. A labor of love and more—devotion, fervor, desperation?

"The great accomplishments of the Korean people," Miss Ahn, the tour guide, said.

"What are you smiling at?" You joined me on the periphery of the crowd.

"Why do you care?" I said.

"You're mad at me."

"I'm just looking like everyone else. Why ask me? Ask her," I said and pointed to a girl in a clump of boys and girls a few feet away from me.

"Why can't I ask you?"

"I'm trying to listen to Miss Ahn," I said and moved away.

"I can tell you more about this place than she can," you said, following me.

"No, you can't."

"I can."

"I want to hear what she has to say."

"I have something better to show you."

"Not interested."

"But you don't even know what it is."

"I'm busy."

"Okay, sorry," you said. "I'll leave you alone."

"Good."

"Good," you said and walked away, walked away to Lloyd.

My cheeks felt hot. I wanted to cover them and run off, but there was no place to go. I tried to pay attention to Miss Ahn, but all I could hear in my ears was your voice. *I have something better to show you.*

My cheeks were still flushed when you returned a few minutes later. "I'm sorry, okay? Whatever I did, I'm sorry."

I was thrilled to see you, but I didn't want to show it. I looked up at the Buddha instead. "Can't believe human beings actually made something like this. It's incredible."

"Ridiculous waste of human energy and monument to human enslavement, you mean."

"Enslavement?" I raised my eyebrows at you.

You had a beautifully earnest face. "Lloyd said this was built by slaves in the Silla Dynasty—even up through the Joseon Dynasty, they had slavery."

33

"But they don't mention that anywhere."

"Let me show you," you said and took my hand. A small current shot up my arm at your touch and calmed itself as we walked. I loved the nearness of you. You said, "If you think this is fascinating, wait until you see this."

"You're so sure of yourself," I said, keeping my voice light in case you thought I was mocking you.

"Lloyd says he hated me when he first met me. I can be annoying. It's true."

"You're not annoying."

"Yeah, I am. I know it."

"Lloyd doesn't know everything."

You thought about that for a second and nodded. "He's a good guy."

We escaped from the group. It seemed that way. An escape. In a few minutes, we were back out in the giant plaza surrounding the temple. It was breathtaking. How many people must have filled this plaza at one time?

"Better, right?" you said. I couldn't disagree.

You pointed to a group of women on their hands and knees scrubbing the flagstones. They wore maroon kerchiefs on their heads, matching maroon-colored skirts, and light-gray blouses. Over their mouths and noses were white masks, the kind surgeons wear, only these were made of cloth. There were dozens of these women spread throughout the plaza on that hot summer morning, without relief from the sun. I'd seen them as we'd walked up from the bus and thought how quaint they were in their colorful clothing, how they looked as though they belonged in that expansive plaza as if frozen in time. I'd seen them as props, like I'd seen pilgrims at Plimoth Plantation on a field trip once. As we approached the group closest to us, I could see that they were using rags to scrub the stone. They were actually working, and working hard. I could see sweat on their faces as we drew closer, sweat and deep grooves in their leathered faces.

I stopped when it seemed we were impolitely close, but you kept going and knelt beside one of them. You whispered something to her, and she laughed and playfully hit your leg in admonishment, then pulled down her mask. I saw you slip something into her hand, and she looked at it and hit you some more. In that moment, I saw the gray-green of an American bill. "Chamna, cham," she said in exasperation. I heard another woman call out to her, and she answered in Korean, "This fool boy thinks we need whiskey."

All of them laughed. She shook her head, stood up, and started to chase after you to give the bill back to you, but you dodged her like a dancer. Red-faced and toothlessly smiling, she folded the bill into her blouse. "Take care of yourself, eh, auntie?" you said in perfect Korean. Then you went around and proceeded to give all of them a bill here and there until you turned your pockets inside out to show them you had no more.

"Hey," you said to me. "Come on." And you took my hand again and started walking backward, eyes on me again. The women were still shaking their heads as we left that large plaza, back on their knees, shaking their heads and watching us walk away.

"They're laughing at you," I said.

"So? Is that so bad?"

"What you gave them isn't going to change anything for them. They'll still be scrubbing rocks for tourists."

"Every bit helps."

"I don't believe it."

"Yes, you do."

"You're going to trip," I said, but you grinned and kept backing up.

"You'll hold me up," you said.

"Or you'll pull me down with you when you fall."

"Would that be so bad?" You winced.

I thought you were leading me to something, something for which we'd get into trouble. Maybe I wanted to get into some sort of trouble even then. With you, Jaesung, the boy with the empty pockets who walked backward into the future.

"Hey, watch out, a step," I said, and you stopped suddenly and tugged me to you. I was too close to your face, and we were on a step, and we could lose our balance, and that's when you kissed me, and when you pulled away I leaned forward and kissed you back. We tottered on the edge of that step, and then you braced yourself on the next step, and what they say about kissing is true. I gave in to a magnetic, delicious force that pressed our mouths together.

31

I never saw my parents kiss, never saw them embrace. My father patted my mother's arm with tenderness, I could admit that. And she handed him things, like his coat when it was snowing outside or a glass of iced tea on a hot day. And in the transfer, I saw love. She loved him. I saw Willa kiss boys, plenty of boys, at our front door or on the porch swing. And now I understood the attraction. But unlike my sister, I only wanted to kiss one person—and that person was you. And I was afraid I was more like my mother in that way than my sister, and I was afraid love was a trap.

32

You weren't afraid of getting lost. You ran toward it. A new adventure, a surprise around every corner. "I heard there's a town nearby," you said.

We were standing near the gate of the camp in Korea. That morning we'd gone to another Buddhist temple, and it was the first afternoon we had free time. Some on the tour lined up to call their parents in the States on the landline; others lazed around in the range of tall fans. It was hot. There wasn't much relief in the shade. You kicked at the ground. The humidity felt ten times thicker than the mosquito nets we slept under each night. We swatted at flies.

"Right now? Just walk out?" I said, wiping sweat off my neck with a bandana.

"There's a bus," you said.

"It's against the rules," Lloyd said. "They're showing a movie up in the big hall—let's go to that."

"Rules? This isn't school or jail," you laughed. "I'm tired of the propaganda-machine tour. Come on." You held out your hand. "No one will even know we're gone." I took it but stood still, uncertain.

"I can't get into trouble," Lloyd said.

"What can they do to us?" I said.

"Exactly," you laughed. "What can they do?"

I had asked the question in all seriousness, but you gave me such a conspiratorial smile, as if it was the two of us against the world.

"What if we get lost? We don't have a map," Lloyd said, kicking at pebbles.

"How do you think the people who work here come every day?" you replied. "You talk about all this fake stuff they're showing us, this camp that's like a prison, but you don't go out into the real world when you've got the chance? Out there is the real thing. What are you really afraid of, Lloyd?"

Lloyd squirmed, looking at the gate and then back at the Great Hall. He looked miserable. I squeezed your hand. "We should get going if we're going to go," I said. As long as I was with you, everything would be fine. I didn't care about Lloyd, and maybe to be truthful I preferred being alone with you anyway. But you threw him one more plea. "Trust me, it's going to be all right." Lloyd let out a loud breath and started for the gate. I rolled my eyes at him, but you grinned and put your arm around me, and your step was light. You clapped Lloyd on the shoulder when we caught up to him, and I felt him lean into us.

You were right, of course. At the end of the road, we came upon an old bus creaking along, looking as if it would break down. It looked like a model of a bus we had in the States in the 1960s, and I wondered if it wouldn't be faster for us to walk, but you waved it down and we boarded. Lloyd pulled out a few Korean bills from his pocket, to which I added a couple more, and we held them up to the driver. He took the money without counting. I pulled my bandana up over my nose and mouth. The bus smelled like fertilized dirt and garlic and pipe smoke. People stared at us with open mouths, some of them with gaps between their teeth, young and old alike. We pushed our way to the back, where there was an empty spot on the bench seat. I sat in your lap while you and Lloyd squished together. Even though we weren't going any faster than when we'd walked, I was glad to be out of the sun. Your arms were around my waist, and I thought how I shouldn't worry. You were grinning the widest grin I'd ever seen. *Our adventure,* I thought.

The bus took us into a large town. We got off when everyone got off, at what seemed to be the busiest street. You were right about the tour not showing us this town. I hadn't known it existed. People stared at us, and you smiled at them, said a few words in greeting. Lloyd shook his head. "Jaesung loves being a celebrity. Everywhere we go he has to greet his fans," he said to me. I moved away. You'd never criticized Lloyd, and here he was trying to get me to side with him against you. I pretended I hadn't heard him.

I remembered the women cleaning the plaza. You were interested in people, in their everyday lives. You knew they were staring because we wore American clothes, because we were different from them, and you wanted to let them know you saw them. I remembered you and Lloyd at the airport. Lloyd hadn't seemed to dislike the attention back then.

There was a restaurant across the street. I caught up to you and pointed it out. Lloyd followed, and I wished we could have ducked inside without him, but you held the door and tried to cheer him up by making a joke about eating better here than anywhere else so far and how much Lloyd appreciated good food. Lloyd refused to smile.

Inside a fog of cigarette smoke hovered just above eye level. A woman at a table was spooning filling into dumpling wrappers to make mandu. Her full skirt was wrapped between her legs into temporary pants, her knees drawn up so that even though she sat in a chair, crouching, her feet were beneath her on the seat. She waved us toward the back and then returned to making mandu. People from other tables stared at us but then went back to their conversations. We found an empty table in the corner near a large table with a ring of young men who looked to be our age. They studied us as we took our seats, then resumed talking loudly. As the waitress neared, one of the men caught her arm. I saw her roll her eyes with exasperation at him, but she took down his order before sliding short ceramic cups of barley tea on the table toward us.

"Service is too slow here. We should find another place," Lloyd said, staring at the waitress while she wrote down an order from another table nearby.

"Go ahead if you want," I said, hoping he would. His staring at the waitress like that made me uneasy. "We'll meet you back at the bus stop in an hour."

"We've got to stick together," you said. "We'll get something fast, like the mandu that woman up front is making. It looks good." You had your arm around me and moved me closer to you and away from the table with the men, but I could sense that you were focused on their conversation. Their voices became louder; they were arguing. I heard one of them say in Korean, "They'll stop at nothing. Those fishermen disappeared."

"That's straight kidnapping. That's the kind of thing North Korea is going to do," another replied.

"This is taking too long," Lloyd grumbled, farthest away from those men.

Someone pushed back his chair at the table next to us and scraped the rough-hewn wooden floor. I winced and counted six men, all with the same haircut and open-necked button-down white shirts. They were in a heated debate, cutting each other off. Some leaned forward, and others held them back. "That's why his brother joined the student movement," a man said. "Mine too. My brother too."

Someone knocked a teacup on its side, but it was ignored, and a puddle formed on the table. One man's sleeve was soaking in it, but he was oblivious. Their voices rose in a crescendo of disagreement. "Yah," he yelled and then said something in Korean I didn't catch because you pulled me even closer to you, away from them. Then the tension eased. I heard a few men laugh. But the one who had spoken about his brother wasn't smiling.

"I'd be upset too if my brother died that way," Lloyd said. I didn't realize he'd overheard them until then.

"He's not upset about that," you said.

"He just said his brother set himself on fire." Lloyd's eyes were narrowed, and he shook his head. "They jumped out of a building that way."

"The media didn't cover it, so it was wasted. That's what he's talking about." Your arm tightened around me.

"That's what the other guy is talking about, but look at him, Jaesung. He said, 'Dongsaeng.' It was his little brother, and he couldn't stop him."

"Wait," I interrupted. "What happened?" You removed your arm from my shoulders and leaned toward Lloyd.

"It's a protest for the world to see," you said, and I could tell you admired them for it. I felt nervous. It was warm in the restaurant, but a coldness clawed at me.

"They actually think this crazy dictator who's already killed thousands of his own people gives two shits about kids wrapping themselves in kerosene-soaked sheets, setting themselves on fire, and jumping out of buildings? He's laughing at them. Fewer people to deal with." Lloyd's voice was grim.

"At least they died for something," you said in a quiet voice, looking calmly at him.

"But look at his brother, Jaesung," I said because I was beginning to agree with Lloyd. What good did being a martyr do for the ones who loved you?

The man at the table who had been speaking had his head in his hands. The men around him were still arguing, but he was shaking his head now, and the chill expanded in my chest.

You refused to look. "Extreme situations call for extreme responses."

"You can't change anything if you're dead. Who's going to be left?" Lloyd said.

"Lloyd's right," I said. "It's harder to stay in the fight and keep trying to make changes than to quit."

"Harder?" you said in disbelief. "Quit? You think it's easy to die that way?"

"No, I don't mean it's harder." I tried to explain, but the way you looked at me, the look that said I'd betrayed you, made it harder to find the right words. Maybe I did mean "quit," because I related more to the man whose brother had died than to the man who had killed himself. I stumbled, stammering, "I don't mean that. Wait, I mean," and then I found my stride. "I mean you said yourself there's so much to be done. Chun is a dictator. I mean we can go back to the States and get the word out so our government puts pressure on Chun to change. The Olympics are going to be here in three years. If people knew back in the States what was happening here . . ." I threw back at you all the things you'd said to me.

"But people are dying right now. It takes something big to make big changes, or it's more of the same bullshit," you insisted. "Thousands were massacred in Gwangju, and the US, our government, did nothing.

41

They helped Chun to do whatever he wanted so it could be business as usual in Korea. His men are armed with US weapons."

"Because they don't want Korea to become communist like North Korea," Lloyd said.

"Chun can do anything as long as he's America's puppet, and people will continue to suffer here. No workers' rights, no rights for anyone here," you said.

"But how's being a martyr going to change that?" I said.

"It's going to show people how bad it is. The world needs to see, and how else will they see?" You were adamant. Your face was flushed, and I thought this was our first fight, and I wouldn't lose you to something like this. I could see you in a shroud of white, and I felt you were telling me you would do this no matter what I said.

"But the media isn't paying attention, because the media is controlled by Chun's government," I said. "You just said that man's brother died for nothing."

"That's what he said." Your voice was calm again. "Doesn't mean it's true."

"Yoona's right, you've said so yourself. Why are you getting all suicidal on us now?" Lloyd said, using a different tack. Scorn was in his voice. It broke through something in you.

"What do you think should be done, then?" you said to Lloyd. Your hands were flat on the table on either side of your teacup. I wanted to stroke your imperfect finger, hold it to my heart, and beg you to promise you wouldn't ever do what that man's brother had done, for me, promise.

"Work with Tongsu Cho," Lloyd was saying. "Go to the meetings he talked about when we get back to Seoul. There are many paths to revolution, remember he said that." Lloyd sounded reasonable.

I hadn't heard the name before. "Who's Tongsu?" I said.

"Cook at the camp. I'll introduce you to him," Lloyd said to me. Our eyes met. I saw in them the same fear I had in mine. We loved you. I wondered why I'd ever disliked him.

"I like that. 'There are many paths to revolution,'" I said. I felt your eyes on me, taking in the way Lloyd spoke to me and my reply.

"Big and small paths," Lloyd said.

"For people who have all the time in the world." You scoffed.

Lloyd let out a halfhearted laugh. "Whatever, Jaesung. Revolutions take time. You've said so yourself."

You pushed back in your chair as if you had to put some distance between us, as if Lloyd and I had ganged up on you. Not angry, just resigned and maybe resentful.

"Come on," Lloyd said, and I was relieved. "We should go back. That bus took forever, man, and they'll start looking for us." I looked around for our waitress. How much did our tea cost?

But you weren't ready to let it go. "Always following the rules. What the hell are you afraid of?" you said in our direction. There was an edge to your voice, and Lloyd jumped on it. And we were back to arguing again.

"Afraid? I'm not afraid. Just because I don't want to burn myself up, you think I'm afraid? Because I disagree?" He stood up and leaned toward you, his hands on the table. "I'm not allowed to disagree with you? You don't know what it's like to really take a stand on anything. You and all these fucking people don't have a fucking clue."

The hum of voices in the mandu shop suddenly stopped. The ring of men at the table beside ours and the people at the other tables were looking at us now.

You were looking into your cup and turning it round and round with your hands. I could see then that you were determined to jump like that man's brother had jumped, and nothing Lloyd or I could say would change your mind.

Lloyd's face contorted as if he were holding back a flood of words. It was barely a second, but time seemed to stop. I took a sharp intake of breath.

43

I thought for a second that he was going to punch you. Instead, Lloyd jumped up, his chair overturning on the floor behind him. And then his arm swung out, and he snatched up your cup and threw it on the stone floor at your feet. It shattered into pieces. I saw from the look on Lloyd's face that he had startled himself with what he had done. And then he was gone. You called to him to come back and went after him. I apologized to the waitress, who was suddenly beside me, righted the chair, gave her money for the tea, and then excused myself.

My heart was in my throat. That's a saying, and that would be the accurate feeling. I didn't know what I'd find outside. In the early evening sunlight, Lloyd had his back to the low stone wall of the building that housed the restaurant, the curled tiles of the roof above him, and you were in front of him. You had your hand on Lloyd's shoulder, and you talked to him in a low voice. "You're right, you're right, you're right," you said. "I'm sorry, I wasn't thinking when I said that."

Lloyd's hands were fisted in front of his eyes. At the time I thought he was as upset as I was at the thought that you wanted to be a martyr. I thought he'd succeeded in convincing you to discard that option, and I thought his outrage had made all the difference, because you didn't mention it again. I saw Lloyd differently after that. I saw him as a friend.

33

I didn't know how lonely I was until I met you. Isn't that the way of love? Don't all lovers say the same thing? Everything changed after they met, the sun was brighter, the sky suddenly announced itself: *I'm here, I'm here.* Everything suddenly mattered, I came into existence, no longer running between my mother and father, no longer Willa's sister who cleans up the mess in the kitchen after a fight, I was seen all on my own. You looked at me, and I suddenly materialized into a physical being, all of me. Your hands on my skin reminded me I was alive. And even when we argued, you allowed me space to argue, and you were never loud. You said, "Let's talk about it. Do you want to talk about it?" And you said afterward, no matter what I'd said or done, "I'll always forgive you." No one had forgiven me before or asked me to forgive them.

34

My promise to myself before I met you was that I would never be in love with anyone. In love, as in at the mercy of emotion. In love, as in unable to leave you if I had to, even if you turned out to be abusive like my father. In love, as in unable to think about anything else when you're not with me. In love, as in making a fool of myself and telling you everything, even if you'd think I was the worst person in the world. The wishing-I-weren't-in-love kind of love; the desperate kind; the hook, line, and sinker sort of love; the out-of-control kind.

I told you we should break up. I told you to keep your distance. There were plenty of people on this tour, so we didn't have to be beside each other. I told you we should do it now while it was still possible. And you looked at me and said, "Why?"

This was the fight we had after we visited the Emile Bell on the student tour. The "mommy" bell, the bell that celebrated the child thrown into the molten lava so her father could make a bell that pleased the king. The story of this child triggered something in me. I couldn't tell you about my mother and father and what it was like to grow up in a house they fought in. Instead I told you I never wanted to see you again. And you said, "You're kidding. Over what?" And I said, "You don't understand. You'll never understand." And you said, "Try me." And I said, "No."

But the next day I waited for you outside your cabin, and I said I was sorry, and you said, "I still don't understand." And I said, "Even so, can you just forgive me for yesterday?" And you said, "I forgive you. I'll always forgive you."

Three times in two weeks I said I'd never talk to you again. And each time I went back. There are songs about this kind of desperation. Fairy tales. Cautionary tales. Lloyd talked to me during those times. He said, "Jaesung doesn't understand when people have to be by themselves. You need space. I get it." And I said, "Look after him for me?" and he agreed he would.

After the third time, I had to promise you I'd never break up with you again. Not like this. "Promise me that. We'll always be friends, even if you decide you don't want to see me anymore. Not this kind of shutting the door. Not this way where you say we'll pretend we don't know each other. I can't take that, I'm telling you. Promise," you said. I promised. I didn't resist. I couldn't.

35

Lloyd cocks the handgun and holds it over Heather. YOU NEVER LIKED ME. AND SINCE WE'RE BEING HONEST, I NEVER LIKED YOU EITHER.

Negotiate. A voice is screaming in my head. *Say something. Now. Negotiate, Yoona.* You'd do that. My mother did that. Even Willa, in her own way, with her avoidance, was finding a way to handle our volatile father. Up until now I've resisted looking at Lloyd head-on. This isn't going to end soon.

"If you shoot her, they'll hear, and they'll come in and kill all of us." It's Faye's voice.

THAT MEANS THEY'D BE RESPONSIBLE FOR KILLING ALL OF YOU. I THINK THEY'LL TRY TO SAVE ONE OF YOU AT LEAST. He steadies his shaking hand and aims the gun at Faye on the bed next to me.

"Lloyd, okay, no bullshit, you're right. Let's be honest, I have that problem. You know what Jaesung said, I shut you out, and I was wrong. I should have gone with you. What are you saying about proof that Jaesung is alive?" I say as loud as I can.

I swear it's nearly a smile on his face, a smile and relief. I've seen it before, and if I have to pretend one more time, I'll do it For my friends' sakes, I have to do it. This has gone too far. Too far, and I can see that there's no going back now.

He turns to me. I have to look straight back at him. There's silence. Even Daiyu has stopped crying. They wait.

36

During the second week of the tour, we went to the DMZ. A man in a beige uniform greeted us and explained that there were thousands of US army, navy, and air force soldiers combined in one place on the southern side of the 38th parallel. "Together with our army, the North knows they can't invade by land. But they will stop at nothing," he said, his voice louder now. "We always have to be on guard. Which is why," he said, "they try to get to our shores at night. Which is why they've infiltrated our universities and factories. Those communists will even go overseas to other countries to kidnap people who are on our side.'

He took us upstairs to a guard tower, where another man in a beige uniform handed us his binoculars. I looked across the field in the direction he pointed, at a town he'd said had been made up to look like a common village but was a stage set. Propaganda. You were quieter than everyone else. Lloyd was arguing with one of the tour guides, Mr. Kwang, about something North Korean. But you stayed away from them. You looked out into the distance and didn't comment.

After that, the spokesperson said he wanted us to see how the North Koreans had begun to infiltrate—he was going to show us proof of it. They'd nearly made it all the way to Seoul, he claimed. We'd go down into the tunnels the South had dug to intercept the North's tunnels. I didn't need to see any more. All the uniforms and weapons and talk of invasions were making me nervous. What were we doing here?

At the entrance of the tunnel they led us to, I held my breath. The earth. The roots in it. As we walked, I stayed close to the middle of the tunnel, the tallest part. Away from the sides, covered with the root strands of the underbrush and trees. The tunnel widened as it leveled out. I told myself there was plenty of room for all of us and tried to keep moving. The guides were shouting at us to keep up. People around me were chatting, but it was in hushed tones.

I could imagine soldiers from both sides storming through these tunnels, coming at us with bayoneted guns while we cowered, trapped in the middle. I wouldn't be able to go forward or backward. When I finally let out my breath, the smell of dirt and insects and sweat and smoke filled my nose, and a metallic taste filled my mouth. Was something burning? The walls suddenly felt close to me, as if they were by my ears—was that possible? Had they narrowed like that? I closed my eyes, but I could feel the wispy roots of trees and hear boots pounding through the tunnel, see men in uniforms with rifles pointing at me. I'd be shot and trampled. My feet stopped. I couldn't go any farther. The rest of the tour group walked around me. Some walked into me, not knowing I'd stopped. How were there so many of us? I took a step backward, and someone protested before passing me. Soon they'd all pass me, and that thought frightened me as well. Which was worse? To be with all of them as we were killed together or to be caught by myself, trying to flee? I took a step backward.

"Ready to leave?" It was you. "I pretty much get the idea of these things, don't you?" you continued.

"As much as I need, anyway," I replied, relieved as we retraced our steps back to the mouth of the tunnel.

"Can only take so much propagandist bullshit."

In minutes we were back out in the sunlight.

"Looks pretty real to me," I said, looking back at the tunnel. "How's it propaganda?"

"Do you think North Korea really made those tunnels?"

"Why would they lie?" I asked.

"Serves their story, don't you think?"

"North Koreans are the bad guys?"

"Think about it," he said.

"It has to change in our parents' lifetime," I said. "My father was separated from his whole family. He was only fifteen years old. He wants to see them again before he dies. I can't imagine never seeing my parents again."

"I'm sorry for him. My parents' families came down together." Jaesung kicked at the ground.

"Lucky."

"But they have their own issues. I wonder sometimes if it serves other countries for Korea to be like this, separated."

"You mean the United States and the Soviet Union."

"Someone's benefitting from it. Lloyd says there's evidence. When we get back to Seoul, we're going to talk to some people. Tongsu Cho is going to work for a restaurant there. He said to look him up. He's going to introduce us to some people behind the scenes."

"The cook Lloyd talked about?"

"We'll see what's really going on."

37

BUT IF YOONA TELLS THE TRUTH, I'D HAVE TO THINK ABOUT IT. YOU READY TO TELL THE TRUTH NOW?

"The fuck," Faye shouts at me. "Tell him what he needs to hear." Lloyd smirks at her, walks over to me, and sits. I look down at my taped wrists, which are pinched red from the strain.

"He's crazy. Nothing she says will change his mind," Heather mumbles.

SHE KNOWS WHAT I MEAN. Lloyd nudges me with his shoulder as if we could be any two friends teasing each other. GO ON. TELL THEM.

I force myself to speak with as much truth as possible. "I'm saying I was wrong. You're right. You never gave up on Jaesung, but I did. He told me you were his best friend. I see why now. I see you've been fighting by yourself all this time. Even in Korea, it was you and Jaesung who fought together on the same side."

38

Lloyd kept his promise to me in Korea about Tongsu Cho. He found me in my cabin, folding my mosquito net. I'd missed lunch and dinner, having been curled over since we'd returned from our morning tour of another Silla palace. My stomach had been cramping, so I'd been running to the bathroom over and over again, having eaten something that made me queasy, probably too much of the hamburger and fries they'd given us for breakfast. (We had American food for breakfast and Korean food for lunch and dinner. The cafeteria staff didn't distinguish between types of American food, since Korean food was not categorized by meal time.) When I asked about you, Lloyd hesitated.

"Is he sick too?" I said, picturing you as miserable as I'd been, crumpled over on your yo.

"Different kind of sickness." He had his hand on the ladder to my bunk.

"How bad?" There was a small fan on the wall nearby, and I thought I'd heard him wrong.

"Forget it. You should be hydrated. Tongsu Cho can make you juk. Can you walk to the kitchen, or should I bring it back for you?" He peered up at me.

"No, no, I can manage," I called down. "What about Jaesung?"

Lloyd backed up as I climbed down the ladder. He didn't answer me. The sunlight was bright outside even though it was nearly seven thirty in the evening.

"What was for dinner?" I said and then stopped him. "Wait, don't tell me. The thought of it will make me throw up."

"You look a little greenish," Lloyd replied, concern on his face.

I touched my cheek with my hand. I'd brushed my teeth an hour earlier, after I'd thrown up. Maybe I wasn't ready to eat anything yet. But where were you? I hoped you'd sent him to check on me. I had been feeling sorry for myself and missing you, hearing the girls in the cabin fuss about what they were up to. No one had offered to help me. Instead they treated me as if I had a contagion.

"You'll see him soon," Lloyd said, and I was grateful. We'd been together at some point every day for nearly two weeks by then. An entire afternoon and into the evening seemed like eons.

"He went to town again, didn't he?" I said as a fear rose in me. "On the bus, is that where he went? Would he try to talk to those men in the mandu shop?"

"Nah, he's here," Lloyd said. "You sure you're able to make it to the kitchen?" He warned me about the step before the doorway as I stumbled toward it.

"I haven't ever been this sick," I told him. "Please tell him not to worry."

Lloyd let out a breath, looked down at his sneakers. "Okay, he's with a girl. She's in the cabin next to yours, but it's not what you think, at least not yet."

"What do you mean by that?" I stopped short.

"Her cousin told her he's going to join the martyrs, so it's really about that. Jaesung says he wants to support them, but I don't know. He's still obsessed with the idea of jumping." He slid the door open to the Great Hall and waited for me to enter first.

"But he said in Seoul we'll go to meetings and—" I didn't finish.

There you stood, a few feet away from me. You were engrossed in a conversation with a girl with a hand on her hip. You were nodding and talking, and your hand was out as if you'd catch her if she fainted. You looked earnest, determined, and she was grimacing and talking just as hurriedly to you. You were standing close to her, too close, and then I saw your hand take hold of her arm. She laughed at something you said.

"But it is," you said. "Don't you see, that's the only way anything will change."

She shrugged. "They're going to send him to the States to get away from his friends," she said. You let go of her arm. "Can't blame them. He's their son." You seemed disappointed.

"Yoona needs juk," Lloyd said while I hung back. You looked up at his words, and I saw your eyes brighten when they found mine. "Hey, you're feeling better," you said and rubbed my arm. There was an awkward silence as I searched for a reply.

Finally, the girl held out her hand. "I'm Aecha."

I shook it as Lloyd said, "This is Yoona."

She smiled, putting her hand back on her hip. "You're friends with Cindy Im. From Boston?"

"That's Yoona Sung. This is Yoona Lee," you said while I still couldn't seem to find my voice.

"Ah." She nodded. "Got it." More silence followed. Then she said to you, "Talk to you later?"

"Definitely," you agreed. I wasn't sure I liked the sound of your certainty even though we were all stuck on this tour together.

We watched her walk to a table where a group of girls were polishing their toenails beside a tall fan. I saw her look back as you started to explain.

"I'm going to meet her cousin when we get to Seoul," you said. "Before he goes to the States with her. But I don't think he's going to go. She says he's snuck out twice, and maybe he'll have jumped by the time we get back. She hasn't heard from her family, but she hasn't called. She's afraid to hear."

"Can't you see how fucked up that is? She can't call her family because she's afraid to hear her cousin killed himself?" Lloyd said flat out.

You ignored him. "Have you stopped throwing up?" you said to me. I let you lead me away, and Lloyd trailed after us. There was no reason for me to be jealous of Aecha, was there? I wrapped my arm around you and hugged you close as we walked toward the Great Hall.

The kitchen was behind the cafeteria, next to the Great Hall. Shelves of large pots and pans and bins of bowls and plastic tubs lined the room. In the middle was a wooden table; against the wall sat a huge stove with a small pot set on a burner and large doors of what looked to be refrigerators.

A man was putting away a large colander. He turned when we entered, and you and Lloyd clasped him in high handshakes. Lloyd started talking first, but the man seemed more interested in you, because he didn't respond until you said in Korean, "This is Yoona, she's not feeling well." Then the man's vision seemed to clear, and he noticed me for the first time.

"So this is the young lady," he said in Korean.

I held out my hand in a formal greeting, but he didn't take it. Instead he motioned for me to sit at the table in the middle of the kitchen. "Where is it?" he mumbled in Korean and searched in a drawer until he withdrew a spoon and headed for the stove. He proceeded to stir the contents of a small pot and said over his shoulder in English to us, "Better more time, but what can you do."

You explained that I knew Korean. "Of course," he replied in English. "You have Korean blood—you speak Korean. One people." He nodded at us. "One country. All the same people."

When he placed a bowl of soupy rice in front of me, I saw that his fourth finger had been amputated above the large knuckle. "Factory accident," you said in English, as if reading my mind.

Tongsu Cho held his hand out, fingers spread. "Many, many," he said, still in English.

"He means there were other workers who lost their fingers just like him at the factory," you said.

"That's why he became a cook," Lloyd added. "The factory didn't have any safeguards for the workers—it was routine to lose a finger." Tongsu nodded at me as if confirming Lloyd's words and pointed at the bowl for me to eat.

I spooned some rice and tasted it. The warmth was soothing. "It's delicious, thank you," I said in Korean.

"You speak very well," he said, still in English. And because he spoke to me in English, I figured my Korean wasn't as good as yours or Lloyd's. "Eat more," he gestured. Your hand was on my shoulder, and I wanted it to stay there. I stirred the juk to cool it. Lloyd was talking in Korean.

"Mr. Cho, repeat one more time what you told me this morning."

Tongsu Cho bent his head down, an arm around you and Lloyd in a huddle. In Korean he said, "Who benefits if Korea is two separate countries? Kim Il Sung is a strong leader for the people of Korea. He can't be bought by the United States government, do you understand? No deal." In English he said it again. "No deal. Tough." Then he continued in Korean. "Kim Il Sung is so strong even the Japanese respect him. They're supporting him. They're smart: they know who is going to win, and this is a war—let me tell you—this is a war that will continue, but the North is where the power is, the best factories. My family is from the same area as Supreme Leader Kim Il Sung. If we organize in a smart way, we'll succeed, I promise you."

I ate the juk, which had a rich pork-broth base, as they talked.

"But tell Jaesung where you're going after this," Lloyd urged.

"This is only a two-week job," Cho said.

"Yes, so tell us what you're doing afterward. You know, about Seoul." Lloyd was nodding and blinking as if hurrying Cho onward, as if his nods and blinks were hands on Cho's back, pushing him onto a stage.

Cho took a breath and paused, looking at each of us to see if we were paying attention before he began. "I know a man who knows a man who is Supreme Leader Kim Il Sung's second in command."

"So?" you said.

"So there's going to be a big protest," Lloyd burst out. "Tell him, Mr. Cho, tell him."

"Oh, that," you said, seeming dejected. "You already told me about that."

Lloyd leaned forward. "But this one, this one's different. He just told me this today. Tell him," he implored Cho.

Cho shook his head. "I don't know if it's different, but there are leaders who need our help. One in particular who can unify our country."

You were suddenly alert. "Kim Dae Jung?"

Cho inspected my bowl. "Don't like?" he said in English.

I replied in Korean, "I do. It's good, thank you. You gave me a lot, that's all."

"Come tomorrow, I'll give you more. It'll be better next time," he said in Korean and smiled at me. I felt his approval.

"Will you be meeting with Kim Dae Jung, Mr. Choi? Is that the secret in Seoul? Are you planning something with him?" you said.

Lloyd was nodding again. "I told you, Jaesung. Forget the martyrs. There's work to do."

"We'll meet you in Seoul, wherever you say," you said to Cho, who was wiping down the stove with a sponge.

"They'll be checking your cabins. You should go," Cho replied without looking up from his work.

"Tomorrow. Will you tell us tomorrow?" you said.

"If you're interested," he said, his head still down.

"How come you never told us before, Mr. Cho?" you asked.

"You never asked before," he said. "Carry this cabbage to the back room?" He pointed to a large box on the floor. You and Lloyd bent down to lift it and left me in the kitchen alone with Cho, who lost no time in signaling for me to come closer to him. I thought he had a task for me like the one he had for you and Lloyd, but he didn't. He looked at the doorway through which you'd carried that box with Lloyd and said, "Jaesung is too idealistic."

I wasn't sure what he meant, because he was speaking now in Korean.

"I'm only a cook," he continued. "Before that I operated a machine that made tin boxes. Do you understand what I'm saying?"

"Did you lie just now?" I asked in Korean. "Were you lying about knowing Kim Dae Jung? Did Lloyd ask you to lie?"

He looked me in the eye. "We have to protect our friends."

We heard footsteps nearing. You were on your way back already.

"I have advice for you," he continued in Korean. "A woman between two men is not good for anyone, especially the woman."

"Lloyd and I are friends. You don't understand. I'm not between anyone," I said.

You and Lloyd returned to the kitchen, and Cho said loudly, still in Korean, "Second advice: don't drink cold water, even if it's hot outside. Drink barley tea. It's been boiled. The hamburger didn't make you sick."

I nodded. And then Cho shooed us out of the kitchen, and he was right to, because a tour guide was in the Great Hall as we made our way back, and she barked at us to get to our cabins.

39

AND WHAT ELSE? It occurs to me that the shotgun Lloyd laid across his knees holds the clue to how to get us out of here. I've seen it before somewhere. Did Lloyd have it with him when he came to Weston the first time? I can't remember, but I feel I should. I should know. A warning I regret not registering. It is a feeling akin to sensing rising rainwater in our basement the summer I was seven years old, when I went down the creaky stairs to get the orange bucket of pollywogs Willa and I had caught in a pond in the woods, hoping to see them turn into frogs. But it had already rained too much, the basement had flooded, and the bucket floated sideways. I hoped some of the pollywogs had escaped, even as I saw many motionless in the water. Willa said they'd died earlier in the night, probably, and not because of the rain, but I didn't believe her.

40

"He'll talk your ear off," you said about Lloyd, "but he's smart and knows a lot about the history here. His parents wouldn't have let him come, but he won a trip from a Korean company that was offering them—public relations thing—to college students. I think he had a rough time of it in high school. He's a little extreme—odd, you know—but when you really talk to him, he knows everything. He's read a ton. When you know that much, there's a lot to be angry about. He's a little emotional, but who isn't?"

"You see the best in everyone."

"Everyone has something, right? We all have more than we show the world. Lloyd has a ton under there. He should grow up to become secretary of state or something. He'd make a great one."

"But that's what you want to be," I said.

"Me and him, we'd be co-secretaries of state. Or he could serve first, and then I'd go. So much left to do here and in the rest of the world, so much."

"I wasn't sure about him at first, but now I like him. I see why you're friends," I said.

"He gets emotional," you said.

"Yeah, like at the mandu place," I said with a laugh, and then I said seriously, "You don't want to be a martyr, do you?" And I held my breath.

"Yeah, that was wild. Lloyd's pretty stubborn," you said, and I took that to mean he'd convinced you.

Later that same day, you showed me how Lloyd put a bandage on a girl who had cut her shin on a tree branch. We were on a short hike through a park during the tour. You shook your head. "Look at him. He studied being an emergency technician's assistant so he'll be able to work his way through school. But he got a scholarship, so he doesn't have to worry, but still. He thinks something's going to go wrong. But if he didn't have it, the scholarship, I mean, he'd find a way. Lloyd finds a way. Once you've struggled like that, you never let anything stop you again."

"You sound like you've been there," I said.

"Me? Nope. Nothing like Lloyd."

41

Outside the room, there's the sound of a loud engine, wheels spinning, and men's voices calling. FUCK, he hollers, hugs the shotgun to his chest, and runs to the window.

THERE'S A GODDAMN POLICE TRUCK OUT THERE NOW. SAX WAS BUY-
ING TIME.

"What did you think was going to happen?" I say. Lloyd is rubbing
his face. When he gets nervous, he rubs his face. You told me that in
Korea.

How do I persuade him to let us go?

"I think Sax has a point. The president isn't coming here. We could
go there, go to the White House to talk to him," I tell him.

I WAS WRONG ABOUT YOU. He speaks to me over his shoulder.

I have to switch gears. "You were right to say that. Jaesung said
you'd had a hard time when you were a kid. We talked about everything—like you and he talked about everything. You knew Jaesung
better than I did."

I TOLD JAESUNG YOU WERE ON OUR SIDE. He starts pacing again.
WHAT WERE YOU THINKING, YOONA? HOW COULD YOU DO THIS TO HIM?
TO US? I'VE ALWAYS TRIED TO INCLUDE YOU. I SAID YOU WERE PERFECT
FOR EACH OTHER. I TOLD HIM YOU WERE DIFFERENT FROM THE OTHER
GIRLS. HE WAS INTERESTED IN OTHER GIRLS, BUT I FOUGHT FOR YOU.
WHY DIDN'T YOU JUST GO WITH ME IN THE FIRST PLACE? I KNOW YOU
WERE MAD, BUT LOOK WHAT'S HAPPENED.

I won't believe him. What other girls? Aecha, the girl with the cousin
who was going to be a martyr? Were there others? I feel a part of me crum-
ble inside, but I won't fall apart. Not now. He's wrong. Lloyd is wrong.

"It took me a while, like it's taken me now. Like you, Lloyd, I'm
telling you, I know I made a mistake. Let me help now. Please. If you'd
do this, then you must have proof. What is it?" I stretch my hand out
to him.

IT'S TOO LATE. It's the quietest he's ever spoken since he stormed
into this room. He stops in front of me. His brows shift into confusion,
uncertainty.

"It's never too late. You said Jaesung is still alive out there, and we
can make them release him. How can it be too late?"

I've done too much. He doesn't look at me.

"If you can forgive me, I can forgive you, and so can everyone else, right?" I look to my friends, and they shake their heads in flurried agreement. "Just let us walk out of here. Now. Nothing bad has happened. You got a little anxious to get help for Jaesung faster than it was going. You were frustrated. We all get frustrated."

Lloyd turns the shotgun over several times, but I see he's listening to me.

"Since you have proof now, we can find him, can't we?" I keep my voice earnest and light, not the way I feel with my ankles taped and my wrists hurting. I talk as we had weeks ago in this very room, not as if the police are outside, not as if my friends and I are sitting here at his mercy. I remind him he used to trust me.

You've lied too many times.

"I only lied once to you. I said I was going home the day before yesterday when you stopped me in the quad, and you're right, I didn't go home. But you know it's because you wouldn't leave me alone."

It looks like it hurts. He waves the shotgun at my feet.

"I've got bad circulation. Remember I could never sit on the floor in Korea without my feet falling asleep?" I continue talking. I have to keep talking if we're to have a chance. "Jaesung said I needed vitamin E, almonds, mangoes—which is why he knew what vitamins and food to eat." I didn't mean to move my feet, but I couldn't help it. I hope he doesn't see that they're not bound tight.

If I don't speak to the president, they're going to kill him. I have proof that the men Jaesung was with on the night he disappeared worked as spies for North Korea.

Even though I know you're dead, the vision of you about to be killed makes my heart lurch. Lloyd sounds convinced. I try to smooth out my shaky voice. "Tell Sax you and I will fly right out of the county airport to meet with President Reagan."

But there's no time.

"Faster than all the security required to bring the president here. Come on, Lloyd, this is a college in Pennsylvania. And you're holding hostages in this room at gunpoint."

But once we're out of this room, they'll shoot me.

I speak to the Lloyd I remember from Korea. "You've got to leave this room somehow. The president is not walking in here. Be realistic. What did you think was going to happen?"

It wasn't supposed to happen this way.

"If you didn't come in here with guns and Daiyu looking like this, I would have gone with you."

He stares me down.

"Okay," I say. "You're right. I wouldn't have, but now I believe you. You've made me believe you. I needed to hear you say it. You're right. I'm listening now. Tell me about your proof."

Lloyd walks to the desk and takes out scissors. He knows where everything is in this room. He moves in this jerky fashion, so I can't help but flinch as he approaches, unsure what he's about to do, stab me with them or—and then he grabs my feet and cuts through the tape around my ankles. He's in a hurry, looking back at the window, and doesn't seem to register how the tape doesn't go completely around my ankles. I hold out my wrists so he can cut them too because he's going to release me, isn't he? Instead he shakes his head and picks up the phone and yells into it. I want a car to take me to the airport. Me and the girls. One way to Washington, DC. And I want to meet the president. Clock is reset to one hour. Get me the car. A car and money. We'll need money. A thousand dollars. A car and a thousand dollars. I just want to talk to the president.

I can feel a glimmer of hope spread throughout the room. Between the car and the airport, there's bound to be a way to free us from this lunatic. And he thinks I won't run.

42

You and I were sitting against the chain-link fence in Incheon. The tour group was in the hotel, but we had snuck out. We were returning to Seoul the next day. "Do you believe in curses?" you said. Your question surprised me. You were practical about everything but this.

"It's 1985, Jaesung. Curses are old superstitions. People hurt people."

"My father lost his lower leg in a tractor accident when he was a kid. His brother died of smallpox. His father died in his sleep."

"Any family, especially back in the day, had someone die of things like that. One of my mother's sisters died of smallpox, another one of pneumonia. Surviving childhood was a feat. I'm sorry—those things are horrible, but I wouldn't call that a curse."

"My great-grandfather married a woman who was really sick. It was probably leprosy, my dad said. He cured her of it, which shocked everyone—probably not a cure, but that's what he called it—then he left her to study in China. He wanted to be a scholar and never came back. He was actually detained by a Chinese official, we found out later, but his wife thought he'd run away to start a new life, and she killed herself, cursing him and any children he'd have. There's been nothing but tragedy in every generation since. Like that song 'Arirang,' where the woman says if you throw me away, your feet will get diseased and you won't be able to walk any further."

"But how did he have children if his wife died?"

"He returned to Seoul eventually and married and had two children before he died of a mysterious illness."

"Every illness was mysterious back then."

"True," you said with a laugh. Then you were serious again. "But it's always been that way. As if fate or some monstrous thing was determined to make my family suffer, each one of us. And I know it always will be." You said it so softly, as if you expected the ground to open and swallow you whole for such an admission. As if not saying it too loud would keep it from happening. But then nothing happened, and I tugged at the arms you'd crossed over your chest, and you opened them and pulled me in. And you said, "I want my life to be useful."

And I said, "You think you're going to die?"

"We're all going to die, Yoona."

"But you promised me and Lloyd you wouldn't sacrifice yourself that way." My eyes started to tear.

"Hey," you said and kissed them. "I'm not going anywhere."

"You promise?" I said.

You nodded, and better than a kiss was pressing my cheek against yours and memorizing the way it felt. Our arms around each other. Listening to our breaths. We nestled together against the wind coming off the ocean. "I'm holding you to that promise," I added.

"Do you have something you've never told anyone?" you said.

"Mine is boring," I said. I didn't know about fate, but there were real monstrous things out there to be feared, and they came in the shape of real people doing terrible things to other real people. Not just pronouncements of curses. Someday, I reasoned, someday you'd meet my parents, and I didn't want you to feel sorry for my mother. She'd made me promise not to tell anyone. I could picture it, you meeting my parents, meeting my sister, Willa.

"Boring to you might not be boring to me," you said.

"Trust me, you'll find it boring," I said.

You pressed your cheek farther into mine, and we clung to each other, the clinging becoming a burrowing and hunger and kissing that didn't say enough of what we wanted to say. I wanted to chase that stupid idea you had about the curse out of your head. I wanted to show every bit of you that I had the power to change your mind, because isn't there a saying about that? About curses being broken by love, small and big gestures, small and big love? As long as the real-life monsters stayed away, we'd be safe. I wanted to break the barrier of clothes and skin between us, and you were about to pull my shirt over my head, we would have had sex there on the beach against that chain-link fence, except Lloyd's voice sounded through the billowing wind in the dark. Your name, my name, calling to us. We paused for a second, but then kept going, your mouth on the rise of my breast. My lips on the back of your neck. And I wished for just a few more minutes with you before Lloyd found us. Your hands beneath my skirt. Could Lloyd look for us in the opposite direction? And then I felt the spray of sand on my bare legs, and Lloyd stood in front of us in his sneakers, his hands on his knees, peering down at us. You leaned back, pulled my shirt down. I smoothed my hair out of my eyes, brushed sand off my knees. He said the guides were going room to room, taking attendance.

43

WAIT. Lloyd scrutinizes me. AT LEAST ADMIT WHAT YOU WERE GOING TO DO. Lloyd's chest rises, and then it caves, and he puts his head in his hands. His hair is wet with sweat, and I resist recoiling as he sits with a sigh beside me, rests his head on my arms, which are still bound at the wrists.

Now that my feet have been released and he's talking calmly to me, anything is possible. "Lloyd, let's talk about it another time. Let's get out of here. I'll explain to Sax or whoever."

JUST ADMIT IT FOR ONCE.

"If you have proof, show me."

DO YOU THINK HE'LL FORGIVE YOU WHEN I TELL HIM WHAT YOU WANTED TO DO?

"Do you really have proof he didn't die in Seoul?"

YOU STILL WON'T TELL THE TRUTH.

"I don't know what you mean. If you're trying to free Jaesung and want to speak to the president about it, then focus on that, but please cut this tape off me." I hold out my wrists to him. He pats the scissors in his right hand against the side of the shotgun. Eerie silence, with only the click click click of metal on metal. But I ignore it. It's going to be fine now. I can feel his body relax beside mine.

This will be the shortest crisis Sax has every faced. I'm almost delirious, the high I feel. Relief surges through me. All I had to do was apologize and pretend I believed you were alive. Lloyd is a child throwing a tantrum because no one will give him the toy that he wants. The guns made it a potentially deadly tantrum, but then again, we've been through gunfire before. You, me, and Lloyd. We've seen people suffer around us.

"You have to be reasonable. If they think you're crazy, they're not going to let you near the president," I tell him and try to picture what proof he might have.

YOU'RE STILL LYING TO ME.

"Was it Serena's contact at the embassy? Was it the journalist I met in New York?"

He jerks his head up, jumps to his feet, and whirls toward me. Too close for me to stand up and speak out. YOU STILL PLAN TO DO IT.

"You sound crazy again," I say and look up at him. The angle strains my neck.

YOU'RE TRICKING ME.

"I do believe you, if you have proof . . ." I extend my hands out to him.

The scissors are open in his hands, and I see he's gripping them by the blades, and they cut him. YOU'RE STILL LYING TO ME.

"No, I wouldn't—look, you're hurting your hand," I say.

WHAT?

"Your hand, Lloyd. We were having a good talk. Sit back down," I tell him even as my heart has picked up its pace at the threat in his voice.

You cut me, you bitch. He throws the scissors against the wall opposite us with the force of his entire body. I duck—we all duck as they bounce back and fall to the floor. Then he turns to me.

"I didn't do that. How could I? Look, my hands." I hold out my wrists to him again.

"She's telling the truth," Faye calls out.

You're all trying to trick me. He raises the shotgun and points it at me. But they don't know, do they? They don't know you're planning a murder.

"She didn't do anything to you—you did it to yourself," Heather shouts. Lloyd aims the gun in the direction of her voice.

You think Yoona is such a saint. She'll let you die rather than tell the truth.

I was wrong. He's erratic and makes no sense. All the progress I thought I'd made evaporates. I can see in his eyes that in his desperation he will kill all of us.

What have I done? And then I know this can't be the way it ends. You wouldn't give up. You would reason with him. I've seen my mother reason with my father. From her place on the floor where my father pushed her down, she would beg for our lives. I don't know why, but that's what comes to me now, this image of her.

"Lloyd, think about Jaesung," I tell him.

You don't give a shit about him. You don't give a shit about anybody but yourself.

"That's not true. You said you brought Daiyu in here because you knew I cared about her and Heather and Faye."

Just say it, Yoona.

"I don't know what you mean."

Tell them what you were going to do today.

"So this isn't about Jaesung at all." Tears rise in my eyes. For a few minutes I'd begun to hope. If Lloyd had proof that you were alive—I hadn't let myself hope again until today.

SAY IT. I'LL KILL HEATHER TO MAKE YOU SAY IT. YOU KNOW I WILL.

Heather and Faye and Daiyu are whispering and looking from him to me.

"This isn't about Jaesung being alive at all. You don't even want to speak to Reagan."

I'VE GOT TWO MORE GIRLS TO KILL AFTER HEATHER TO GET TO REAGAN. FIRST, YOU ADMIT WHAT YOU WERE GOING TO DO, AND SECOND, YOU SAY YOU AREN'T GOING TO DO IT NOW BECAUSE I WON'T LET YOU.

"Do you really have proof he's alive?"

I WANT YOU TO SAY IT.

"You want me to keep the baby. Fine. I'll do it. We'll do it. We'll raise this baby together." My voice breaks.

Heather takes a sharp breath. Faye says, "What are you saying?" Daiyu is silent. But I'm watching Lloyd. He squints his eyes at me.

Yes, there's a baby.

44

I believed the end of the tour didn't mean the end of us. I don't know why I was confident of that. We kissed on the bus all the way back into the city. Lloyd cleared his throat a few times when the tour guides walked down the aisle, and we separated, but then when the coast was clear, we returned to it. Swollen lips and heavy breathing and hands under each other's clothes.

"I'll see you soon. Sooner than you want, probably," you said in my ear. We were standing on the sidewalk with our bags at our feet. You stepped back because people were crowding us on the sidewalk. You held up the piece of paper where I'd written my aunt's address and her phone number. I didn't trust my voice, or how suddenly my eyes flooded with tears, and turned toward my aunt's car. There was no reason to believe I wouldn't see you again, and I scolded myself for doubting it.

We sped off, and I kept my head down. The chauffeur had come for me. I was relieved my aunt was too busy to pick me up herself.

I noticed different things this time around. Soldiers stood in groups on the corner on the campus of Yonsei University. They wore black fatigues and had semiautomatic rifles slung over their shoulders as casually as book bags. The chauffeur explained to me in Korean when I asked about them that men in Korea have to serve three years in the military. The men looked like recent high school grads, like me, young and oblivious. And smoking. Like the college students walking around them, they had cigarettes between their fingers. Nearly everyone college age smoked. I saw students being stopped and their bags pawed through by police. I thought I saw you in that crowd even though I knew I'd left you back at the buses.

The next day I went shopping with my aunt. All day I worried you had tried to reach me at my aunt's house. I counted the hours until I would see you again. If we weren't home when you came by, then how would I reach you? My aunt insisted on stopping at a restaurant to introduce me to her friends. My aunt's three friends talked and talked as if they hadn't seen each other in years when in fact they'd visited just days earlier. Finally, we were back in the car, headed to her house. I couldn't tell her about you. There would be so many questions. "Are you catching a cold?" she asked in Korean. I denied it.

"I'm fine," I told her.

"I've got so much planned for us. We'll meet your uncle in Busan this weekend—"

Panic scattered through my bones. "Auntie, I traveled so much on this tour that I'd just like to stay here in Seoul," I said in as firm a voice as I could.

She looked startled. "But how will he see you otherwise? This job has him spending half the week—"

The chauffeur turned suddenly at an intersection, forcing me to lean left into my aunt's shoulder and interrupting her words. Behind us I saw a cloud of dust and people running our way. The chauffeur apologized, making yet another sudden turn. More people ran. There were loud explosions and shouting. We sped up, squeezing between other cars on that street. A few young men in all-black clothes ran alongside us, banging on the roof and side of our car. They had white paste under their eyes and noses. I asked what they had on their faces, and the chauffeur said it was toothpaste, to cut the sting of the tear gas. "Hurry," my aunt urged him.

The chauffeur said under his breath, "Usually they give them a way out of these political demonstrations."

My aunt told him, "Concentrate. Get us out of here."

"Third one this week," the chauffeur said when we were in the clear. My aunt was incredulous. But she called my parents and made the mistake of telling them about the demonstration. "I'll keep her safe," she promised. "What can happen? We won't go to that part of the city again. And Busan by the weekend. Oh, I didn't hear that. Yes, Busan is having demonstrations too? We'll stay here . . ." I was relieved. Maybe the demonstrations would work in my favor, and she would not insist on going south.

But then the demonstration we had driven into appeared on the American evening news, and the phone rang the next morning. My parents had moved up my flight. I begged to stay at least the week, but they said they'd already changed my ticket to the next day. I had no way of reaching you. And now it was the third day since I'd seen you. Maybe you'd lost my aunt's address.

"Tomorrow or next week, honestly what danger are you in? I don't know why your mother married such a stubborn man," my aunt said. "Why aren't you eating anything?"

69

"I've been inside all day," I said. "Need to go out. Would that be okay?"

She put down her napkin. "Of course. Your uncle is going to be so sorry he missed seeing you, but these business trips. And . . ."

The maid came in to say my uncle was on the phone. As the maid brought the phone to the table for my aunt, I stood up and headed for the door. I had to convince my parents and my aunt that I couldn't leave. Not now, not without you knowing. I told myself I'd see you in the States in the fall. You'd told me you'd be a sophomore at Cornell. That was probably only a handful of hours from my school in Pennsylvania. We'd see each other. But the panic wouldn't dissipate. I had to breathe fresh air. Or maybe it was something else, something I knew. Everything inside me told me to go outside.

My flight was leaving the next morning. In my head was a rising refrain: "You'll never see him again. You're leaving, and he doesn't know, and you'll never see him again." I knew it was unreasonable. We'd both be back in the States by the fall. But I couldn't picture you and me together there, and I didn't know why.

My aunt's house had a wall around it. There was a doorbell at the gate. I walked to it and opened it, looking down the quiet street to my left and then to my right. And walking toward me in a black shirt and jeans was you, walking with your head down. I couldn't believe it could be you, at just that moment, with me at the gate. I ran to you, and you caught me in your arms, and we kissed. And I remember thinking, *Of course, this was always going to happen.* Why did I doubt you?

"Where've you been?" I said into your neck.

"Remember the cook from the tour, Tongsu Cho? He's here. I ran into him at a meeting."

"What meeting? I don't understand. I waited for you."

You took my hands and held them between us and looked at me. "You won't believe what's going on, Yoona. Things are going to change. They're organizing at every level. It's a real revolution. Unbelievable, but it's real, and it's going to change. All of it, this country, Yoona. I've got to show you—you won't believe it."

"My parents changed my flight to tomorrow," I said.

You dropped my hands at once and started pacing around me. "But you said two weeks."

"I know, but my dad . . ." I held out my hands, but you waved them off.

Then you stopped suddenly, put your arm around me, and started walking down the street. "I'll show you right now, then. Tongsu said it could get out of hand, but so what? Each one of us counts, right? There are people with everything to lose showing up to demonstrate. We've got nothing, right? We'll do it, go together, okay?" you said and squeezed me closer to you.

I had no idea what you meant, not really. "Okay, yes," I replied, thinking I was going to a meeting, going to hear a speech.

Your arm around me, I walked with you. I pulled away once to look back at my aunt's gate. I didn't want her to worry, but I reasoned I'd be right back. I'd walk with you a bit, and then I'd bring you to the house to meet her, and everything would be fine. I hugged you closer to me.

We're walking down a narrow street in Seoul, and a cab stops for us, and we get in. You give the driver an address. And then you say in a low voice to me, "I don't know what's going to happen, but we've got to figure out a way to stay here longer." All my heart can take in right now is that I'm with you. With you. With you. We'll figure it out. You said so, and I know so. I'll figure it out. "Lloyd's waiting for us," you say, and I'm disappointed for a moment, but I know we'll have our chance later. This is the way it is. I don't mind. You look down at me as if reading my mind and pull me closer to you in the cab, and I think I can keep this memory of us, and it will last.

The cab drops us off in a crowd; it can go no farther. People block our way in the street. You pay the driver, and outside the confines of the car the air is festive. It's as if we're going to a parade. People laugh and clap each other on the back. They welcome each other and hurry along, talking over each other about their plans for their jobs, their families. They come out of shops, the people who work there and the people who own the businesses, together. From what they say, I can see they're hopeful and at ease with each other, determined as they join their neighbors in the street.

Lloyd steps out of a doorway, and we greet him louder than we usually would, so contagious is the palpable excitement around us. "Took you long enough," Lloyd says, but he's not really complaining, because the three of us laugh and stroll deeper into the crowd.

(I know I should have said something to you here. This was my last chance. If I could go back to that moment, I would say something about what we should do if we're separated. I'd devise a plan. But how could I have known? Everything until that moment had been easy. We'd escaped everything. Even the trouble in the tour group with the leaders—we'd broken all the rules, and we'd never had to pay.)

Now everything goes wrong. People are shouting, and it's chaos. Too many people in the street. Where did they come from? And then I hear it: rhythmic chanting. The crowd surges forward, and I'm pushed along with them—pushed to move or else I'll be trampled. The sense is that we're going to a slaughter willingly, though I don't know why we'd face a violent end. I don't know the street I'm on, don't know the district. Street to street, left and then right, and then here into this crowd, accidentally into this crowd. And it's a mistake I can't correct right away. I have to back up. Escape. Something is in front of us. I feel it even if I can't see it. Something ahead. You're to my right, and Lloyd is to my left.

"Something's wrong," you say. You freeze just then, we all freeze. Things come hurtling through overhead and clang hard as they hit the pavement. We scatter from them. Tear gas pours out. Our eyes and throats sting. Everyone starts coughing. We jerk away, the whole crowd of us, flinching, together, one mass too big to scatter. We can only brace ourselves as clouds of yellow smoke rise. I hold my hands over my face. The stench of rotten eggs. I bury my face in my shirt. I'm knocked aside. And suddenly there is space and everyone is running. I drop my hands and nearly lose my balance when someone knocks into me. And then it's as if someone has thrown handfuls of sand lit on fire into my eyes. "Don't rub them." Your voice comes through the screams now, and every which way people are running. I crouch, just want to crouch down and wipe my eyes until they stop burning. But rubbing them makes them hurt more.

And then a bigger panic sets in. I look but can't see my hands. And then I feel your hand pull mine along and someone takes my other hand. Your voice calls for me and then Lloyd's joins in. I'm dragged to one side and then another and then forward. "Slow down," I say as my feet slip. I shout, "Wait."

"Come on," you shout. I feel bodies press against me. I'm too slow. And I'm dragged to a standstill on both sides.

Lloyd shouts, "This way." Which way? I take a step, but I'm locked between you.

You hold me up. I know it's your face in the smoky haze. We must move. We must go. Somewhere. We must run.

"Come on, Yoona," you say.

Then Lloyd's voice: "I'm telling you this is the way."

"It's not."

"The fuck, Jaesung."

"The fuck is wrong with you?"

"Stop it." I can't pull my arms free, and then I'm yanked, my arm rips out of your hand. I reach for you and am pushed to the ground. Bodies in white and black, backs, chests, faces of old and young, mouths turned down, hands up to eyes, shoving, pushing along. And where is Lloyd? I stop. I say, "We can't leave him." And you say, "I'm not. Keep going, I'll be right back." And I tell you to wait, but you're gone.

Suddenly the gas dissipates enough that there is calm for a moment. I think we've made it. There are no more people to push against. Like the car ride with my aunt and her chauffeur that comes to mind, we'll be talking about this afterward and remember how it turned out. We'll be relieved, and we'll be planning our next day. And then I see I'm wrong. How many still in the street? They're crouching. And then I see why they're not struggling anymore.

Before us is a wall of soldiers. They're in black uniforms, so I know they're soldiers. They raise their guns. I see them clearly. Suddenly too clearly. The tear gas matters not at all. I don't know how I know with so many people in front of me. You're nowhere in sight, and I know this is the moment we all die.

Everyone ducks. They crouch and cover their heads, make their bodies smaller targets. We squeeze down to the ground. Beg. Everyone around me turns all at once, so completely at once that they look to be people I've never seen before coming from a different direction, and they run, and I have to turn and run too to keep ahead of them, even though I can't, but those people, they overtake us anyway, and I keep looking back for you. Where are you? The explosions come then. At me. Through me. We're all shrieking. Shrieking. Running and shrieking. But ahead of us are only more soldiers aiming at us.

Doesn't matter who is knocked down by whom. Everyone is trying to save herself, trampling and dodging, using each other as human shields. I see a man drag a woman behind him, pause only to look back and hold her between the soldiers and him. She pummels him, but he doesn't let go. I see a woman shove aside another woman in her haste to get away. I run around bodies picking themselves up on the street, trip on someone's arm, and I think I've lost you forever.

And then there you are. I can't believe my eyes, and I also can't believe I ever doubted I'd see you again. You're helping a man in a business suit who has a gash on his forehead get to his feet. He looks dazed.

I run to you, zigzagging my way, ducking, and you ask the man if he can make it, and in reply the man nods and stumbles away. I pull on your arm, and you follow me, still looking in the direction of the man you helped, who is fine—I tell you he's fine, we've got to go. I don't know where, and then a door opens, and a man urges us inside what looks to be a pharmacy of sorts. We follow him down an aisle as a woman shuts the door behind us. There are other people in the store, nursing cuts and other injuries. The woman who shut the door offers us bandages. You thank her, and then the man who had originally let us in motions for us to follow and opens another door for us toward the back. "Straight and out, through the second door, in the alley. A storeroom. Wait there until it's quiet. Go well," he says to us in Korean.

The sounds of gunfire outside are muffled, and we keep going, following the man's instructions. Across into an alley and then through another and into another building—and you stop and yank me back and tell me it's okay to stop, that it really is okay. We're safe. It's okay. "Let's wait here," you say.

I tell you I thought we were going to die, and the sobs come up from my throat, and we huddle on the floor of a room, a storage room, between crates of vegetables. You say that could never happen.

"Making love" is a strange euphemism. It's more like showing love. It's like words can say only so much. For the rest, there are no words. I've recently finished my period, so thoughts of condoms don't enter my mind, though I know there are other hazards besides pregnancy. We sit up against the door, half-dressed. I trace the scar on your lowest rib, the semicircle, the edge of half a quarter.

"A burn when I was a kid," you explain.

"You were a reckless kid. In the womb with half a pinkie finger, out of the womb with burns." I sigh.

"Enough about me." You raise my face to yours. "Thought that would be more awkward."

"Thanks a lot." I pull back.

"No, for me. It's new to me."

"Haven't you done this before?" I lean toward you.

"It's the truth, Yoona."

"Me too," I confess. "You're the first for me for everything."

You look at me for a long moment, and it is as if I'm seeing a much younger version of you, trusting and eager. And then you say, "Let's do it again." And the enthusiasm makes me believe you really never had sex before.

There is a kind of drunkenness to love. Or illness, as some people have described it. We push and prod, cling and wrestle each other among radishes and onions.

There's an odd quality in that room. We could be in any past century. It reminds me of the first time I saw you at the airport. There was something about you that wasn't of this time and yet was. Nothing pinned you to it. Your close-cropped hair wasn't ancient or futuristic. It had more to do with your face. Or the look in your eyes that seemed to be contemplating something eternal.

We fall asleep. And when we wake, it is dark outside. We dress in a hurry and go outside as if we can fool everyone into believing we were simply walking through that storage room. You pick thin outer layers of onions off my back, and I swipe at dirt on your sleeve. It's astonishing how evidence of the political demonstration has vanished. The street is like every street we saw hours before the protest. Maybe a little dirtier, with newspapers and upturned crates along the curb. I flinch only once when a car horn sounds. Everyone is going about their business around us. We kiss as we walk and run into people on the sidewalk, and some girls giggle at us, and other people tell us to look where we are going, and I don't want it to be night but the sun has gone down. You hail a taxi and put me in it. "I'll find you," you tell me. "As soon as I'm back, I'll call you at Weston."

"I'm jealous you get to stay here," I say.

"Sophomores don't need orientation week," you say. "Freshmen have to suffer." And then you kiss me one more time through the open window, and I push the door open, but you close it firmly again. (Talking about college when we'd just been through a violent street protest seemed out of place, and yet being American students in Seoul during this politically turbulent time did also. I believed our lives would continue, much as they had for other Americans our age.)

45

"You're pregnant, Yoona?" Daiyu asks. I can't meet her eyes.

"Have his baby, for god's sake," Faye says to me. And then to Lloyd, she says, "She said it. She'll have your baby. Let us out of here." She starts sobbing.

Lloyd grabs Faye's arm and shakes it. IT'S NOT MY BABY, YOU DUMB FUCKING BITCH. IT'S JAESUNG'S. I'M SAVING IT FOR JAESUNG, AND WHEN HE'S FREED, HE'S GOING TO THANK ME FOR SAVING HIM, UNDERSTAND? YOUR LIFE IS WORTH NOTHING COMPARED TO HIS AND THIS BABY'S.

I met him when I met you, and if I could not have met him, I could not have met you, so I don't know if I would take it back. He's going to make me take it back. All this is not worth having met you, been with you. How could this have happened to us? Yes, there's a baby. That room after the violent street protest, in that room, when you and I made love among radishes and onions, I got pregnant. And I couldn't do what people do in romance novels or movies. I'm sorry.

"You're mad at me, not her, Lloyd," I tell him. "You're right. I don't want to have this baby, but I will do whatever you want. Let my friends go. I'm the one who shut you out. I was wrong. I'll listen. I'll help. Whatever you want." I put myself between him and Faye. "I'll do whatever you say, just let them go. Please, Lloyd."

46

One night in my dorm room, two weeks after I'd seen you in Seoul, I called you at your parents' house. It was the fourth time in the last two days I'd called and there had been no answer. I figured you'd be back in the States by now and were busy getting ready for college. It was late when I called this time, nearly eleven thirty, but your family lived in North Dakota, so I thought the time difference would make it early enough. Still, I was nervous. Why was I nervous? Part of me remembered the girl named Aecha. Had you left me for her?

"Yes? Hello?" someone said.

I told him I was looking for you, that I was a friend from the Korean tour, and my voice hesitated at the word "friend." Inwardly I was fuming that you were making me embarrass myself this way. You should have called me by now. You should have. But I remembered my promise—no more breaking it off unless I meant it, really meant it, and I couldn't. You knew I couldn't.

I had to ask him to repeat himself because his words didn't make sense. The man on the other end of the telephone line said, "We appreciate your call. My wife and I, it's difficult. We know Jaesung had many, many good friends."

"Is he there? Can I talk to him, please?"

"I'm sorry?"

"I thought he was already back. School started, didn't it? Was there a delay?" I thought how I'd tell you how your father's voice didn't sound anything like yours, and I wondered if you'd sound like him when you were old. I couldn't imagine you old.

"You've caught us at a bad time. We just walked in from the airport. You're asking about my son, Jaesung?"

"Yes, is he there?"

"I'm afraid you don't understand. There was an accident."

"You mean he's in the hospital?" I could picture you now. Of course, you had been in a minor accident and couldn't reach me. "Is there a phone number at the hospital? Could you tell him I called?"

There was a pause. I thought maybe we'd been disconnected. "Hello?" I said. "Hello? Hello?"

Finally, I heard the sound of muffled voices. A low one and a higher one in tone.

Another man came on the line. Sounded older somehow. A deeper voice. He spoke more slowly. "I'm sorry. I'm Jaesung's uncle. There was a car accident on August twenty-first, sometime in the evening, not only a collision but a car fire, and Jaesung didn't make it. We're asking for a little privacy for the family. Friends of his can contribute to a scholarship fund at Lewiston High School and—"

August 21 meant the day after the protest.

I hung up as if the receiver had caught on fire.

47

Your face in the window of the taxi. *I'll see you soon, I promise.* Those had been your words. You closed the door of the taxi. You said you'd find me. You closed the door with your hand on the open window frame of the car, and you said you'd find me. We're intertwined in that little room with radishes on the floor. You said you'd find me. *Sophomores don't need orientation week. Freshmen have to suffer. I'll see you soon.*

48

I remember stillness. Your uncle was wrong. It was as if he'd said I was dead, not you. His words cut my lifeline, and I fell through stillness, fell through space, rolled and rolled, and there was no ground to save me.

49

I sat up all night going over and over it again in my head. I checked and rechecked the phone number I had for you. I called directory assistance and asked them to verify the number I had. And then I called the number again, and the man at your house answered again. Not your uncle, your father. He was kind. He complied. He told me they were all in shock. He said you had many friends. I wanted to shout at him that I wasn't just your friend. I wasn't any friend. "If you want to know, there was no pain. They say it was instantaneous. The car hit them from the side."

"Them?"

"Another boy was in the car with him. He was driving. Jaesung's side was hit, and then the car caught on fire, but they say he was unconscious. He didn't feel any pain."

"Who, who was it? In the car? Who was in the car? Was it Lloyd? Someone named Lloyd?"

"Excuse me a moment." I heard him say something to someone beside him. I heard someone sobbing in the background, noises like sobbing. I heard your father say with his hand over the receiver, "Time for another, darling, doctor said take two pills, good," and then come back to me. Your father gave me the phone number of the other person in the car. "I need to go now. My wife needs me, but thank you for calling." And then he hung up.

Even as I dialed the number, I knew it would be Lloyd's house. Lloyd answered the phone, static breaking up his voice.

"Sorry, do you have a phone number for Jaesung?" I said to Lloyd. "He's supposed to call me, but I haven't heard from him so I wondered if you had. And could you tell him to call me, I mean, when you talk to him?" I said, hearing myself scratch for answers.

"Yoona, they're wrong."

"He was supposed to call me. I think we still have a bad connection, what did you say?" But I didn't really want to know.

His voice suddenly became louder. "Don't believe them."

"No, I just thought he had trouble reaching me, and if you had a number for him—"

"Yoona, he's not dead. I've been trying to figure it out—there must have been a clerical error of some sort. There was an accident, but it wasn't Jaesung who died in it."

"Oh." Relief washed over me. My feet felt to be on solid ground again. Of course there was an explanation. And the mistake would be cleared up. So why hadn't you called me? I told Lloyd about the man I'd spoken to. So that was the reason he thought you were dead. Mistaken identity. Korea was busy and confusing, and it was easy to make a mistake like this.

"Do they know? I can call them right now and ask them about it. They just accepted it, but if they knew the truth . . . ," I offered.

"If I could have stayed longer, I could have shown them."

"His parents will believe you."

"He must be part of something—something big. There was secret service at the meeting we went to, I could tell. They had guns. They could be listening in right now."

"What would they want with Jaesung?"

He was talking rapidly now. "Just promise me that you'll go to your classes and do everything you know he'd want you to do. Promise me. Life as usual. Don't let on that you believe anything other than the official story. Okay? Yoona? His life might be in danger, or we'll be in danger. I've got to go. He's part of some revolution. I saw it, at the meeting."

"Lloyd—"

"Promise me, as far as you know, the official story is he died, okay? Don't let on that you know any different. But there's more, and I'm going to find out. Trust me. Do you trust me?"

I didn't recognize this person who claimed to be Lloyd. His voice sounded like Lloyd's voice, but there was something else too. His voice went flat a few times, as if he wasn't completely there. "Were you in the car with him?"

"I can't get into it now. They could be listening."

"Who's listening?"

"Remember the official story," he repeated.

I told him I would wait.

"Good. If I need your help, will you help me?"

"If it wasn't him in the car, then where is he?"

"We were on our way to a meeting—Jaesung said it was important. Things were going to change because of it, everyone was nervous. So you can't say anything to anyone, promise me."

"Yes."

"Yes, what?"

"I promise."

"Good. Okay, I'll be in touch." And then he hung up.

I didn't sleep that night, but in the morning I went to my classes as Lloyd had said to do. I was numb. But I knew what I'd heard. Lloyd had said you were alive. I held on to that. I didn't feel as if you were gone. I didn't feel a vacuum in my heart like I knew I would if you were dead. Your father's and your uncle's words—those felt like lies to me. By the way, I didn't feel any different. I didn't know I was pregnant. I thought the weepiness I felt was because of you, the pitch and roll of the bed when I was lying in it before I closed my eyes—all that, I thought, was because of you.

50

"Let go of me," Faye shouts at Lloyd.

He holds her one second longer as if to show he can and then throws her away from him. "You're next after that one." He points to Heather.

"A baby, shit, no wonder," Heather says and covers her face with her bound hands.

"No, Lloyd, you can't. If you hurt them, they'll never let us out of here," I plead.

I DON'T CARE IF ALL OF US DIE.

"Yes, you do. How are we going to raise this baby, how are you going to save Jaesung and raise this baby if we die in this room? Come on, Lloyd." I have to convince him.

"You're really pregnant, Yoona?" Daiyu repeats. I still can't look at her. "Why didn't you tell me?"

The phone rings, and Lloyd stands The shotgun falls by his feet. He takes the handgun out of his pocket and begins hitting his forehead with its grip. We wait for him to answer the phone, but he continues hitting himself. Blood appears on his forehead. Will he knock himself out?

51

"Look under the surface, and there's tons more to Lloyd," you had said. "Lloyd knows everything there is to know about Korean history, the history of every country. He's read everything. He's going to be someone important someday. Watch."

That second week in September, as much as I tried to concentrate on my classes, I couldn't stop myself from looking up Korean newspapers in the library, looking up databases for news about Seoul, looking for anything that might tell me about car accidents and political problems, anything at all that might be a clue. But there was nothing. I couldn't get an international line from my phone to ask my aunt about any accidents the day of my flight like the one Lloyd had described. I asked my mother to ask her. And then I called Lloyd again and then hung up after it rang ten times. I reminded myself of your trust in Lloyd. He said you were alive. You had to be alive.

Sometimes I ran into Serena Im, usually around four in the afternoon, when my eyes hurt from looking at the screens and there was something in me that would knock all the machines to the floor if I could, a fear and a restlessness I had to hold in check. You had to be alive. Lloyd said so.

I first met Serena in the stairwell of the student union. I was lost in between the ground floor and first floor. She was looking for a practice room, her cello in a case on her back. I didn't know then that she was *the* Serena Im, musical prodigy, hiding out at Weston College for a year rather than going on a concert tour. She saw a photo of you with me standing at the DMZ fall out of my art history book. She picked it up, held it to her nose. "Bet he smells good," she said. Serena made odd comments, that was true. But she was right. You smelled better than good; you smelled like fresh-cut grass and the sweet grape juice poured into ice cube trays in summer. And in the room with the radishes on the floor where we had sex, you smelled like garlic and cinnamon.

Serena told me things about her parents, who sounded like my parents except her father was a famous violinist, and she said she'd told him to treat her mother better or she wouldn't play cello ever again. "He listened to me for the first time. That's why I'm here," she said. "There's a concert in Seoul next year that he wants me to play in with him, and I've refused. It's his big moment to show me off, all his hard work, but I've told him if there's even a single raised voice at my mother, then it's over. And my brother is my spy at home. He knows he won't get away with it."

Serena and I talked about sex during one of our coffees at the student union. She said, "I met this guy the other day in my music theory class who knows how to have a good time." Leaves fell outside the window like giant snowflakes, big maple leaves, taking their time falling to the ground. It was later than our usual time to meet. I'd opened my book and was reading a section for class while I waited when she appeared. Sunglasses off. Her cheeks flushed.

"Do you love him?"

"Why's that necessary?" She scoffed. "I'm here to learn about the world outside music. That's the goal. I told my parents I want to know what I'm going to miss."

"I thought it was to help your mother?"

"Both. I didn't go to sleepovers or birthday parties, Yoona. I'm seventeen, almost eighteen years old, and I've never gone to a party."

52

"Lloyd, the phone." We're all calling to him, louder and louder, when he suddenly seems to break out of his trance and answers it.

"Everything all right in there?" Sax's voice sounds tinny in the room, but we can make out every word.

Where's our car?

"It's coming. Look, I know you've kept your promise, the girls are safe, but the president's security detail, they're nervous. What is it you want to talk to the president about exactly?"

I don't fucking believe this. I told you: Jaesung Kim, kidnapped August twenty-first outside Seoul in a car fire. Ask the KCIA about it. They know about it.

"That's a serious allegation. A diplomatic solution is required, Lloyd."

My best friend is being tortured in North Korea. An American is being tortured in North Korea. Do you understand? And everyone in South Korea and the United States knows about it. He could die at any time. He could be dying this very minute.

"Stop it." My words tumble out before I can stop myself. I can't stand to hear him talk that way.

"You're saying an American citizen was abducted," Sax says.

You're a part of the conspiracy, aren't you? Sax? Is that your real name?

"Look, we'll find your friend, I promise. Let the girls go, and I'll work with you, I promise."

I'm not giving you the only piece of evidence I have.

"Lloyd, let me see what you have," I say, my heart beating loudly in my ears. Could you be alive?

I don't actually have it, but I saw it. I know what I saw.

"You don't?" My heart sinks. It's just a delusion in Lloyd's head.

Sax is speaking. "Are you still there, Lloyd? Listen, I believe you, Lloyd, but if you can send one of the people in the room out right now, that would go a long way to convince the president's security of your intentions. If you would let at least one girl go right now. What do you say? We'll keep working on releasing your friend in South Korea."

NORTH KOREA. DAMN IT. THAT'S WHY I NEED THE PRESIDENT.

"Right, North Korea. Let one of your friends in the room go so I can show them you mean well. How about it, Lloyd?"

NO ONE HERE IS MY FRIEND.

There's such despair in his voice that I know he means to end his own life. "I'm your friend, Lloyd," I tell him.

He stiffens.

"Lloyd? You still with me?" Sax continues.

GIVE ME A MINUTE. Lloyd looks as if he's counting. His mouth moves: one, two, three, four.

"Just let her walk out of there, I won't send any men to escort her, just let her walk out to us, and we'll get the plane in the air. A private plane for you. That's something I can arrange. And then we'll get you to the White House and go from there. Come on, what do you say?"

HOW DO I KNOW YOU WON'T HAVE A SNIPER SHOOT ME WHEN I WALK OUT?

"Look, it's my job to get you what you want. All of us want this situation resolved. You get what you want. We get what we want. No one gets hurt. Deal?"

Lloyd looks at me. THE BABY COULD HAVE BROUGHT US TOGETHER, YOONA. YOU COULD HAVE INCLUDED ME. I WOULD HAVE FOUGHT FOR YOU.

"What did you say, Lloyd?" Sax's voice.

"I couldn't. I didn't know for sure," I tell him.

THAT'S BULLSHIT.

"Oh, Yoona," Daiyu says, and I can't tell if she's agreeing with Lloyd or understanding that I've said the wrong thing to him because his face reddens.

"Jaesung would want you to raise this baby," I add, because the gun is clenched in his fist. I'm sorry, but I had to say it. Does it matter? Lies will be told in a hundred ways in this room. They already have been.

"Did you say someone is pregnant?" Sax's voice.

Lloyd turns his attention to the phone again and shouts, YOU'RE NOT GETTING THAT ONE.

"That's fine," Sax urges. "It just changes things—if she's really pregnant, we can tell the president. He'll want to know. It's more than four now—it's five, right, Lloyd? There's a fetus. You with me?"

IT'S FIVE. TELL HIM FIVE.

53

My mother explained it to me, as an apology, when my sister wasn't home, that my mother had married a man before our father who lived in her neighborhood in Seoul. I don't know why she thought she had to apologize, but she called it an apology. "I'm sorry, I want to say I'm sorry," she said. "This man, who was very kind, he died right after we were married. There was a terrible sickness that winter, we all got sick, but he didn't recover. I met your father during this time. And we got married sooner than was customary, because he was leaving for the United States. He was never sure about me. That kind of uncertainty can wear someone down. He felt he was second best. And we were too young. I couldn't work with a baby, and I had no family here. If we'd had a little time before the baby came . . ."

"That baby was Willa?"

"No, I lost that baby in the middle of the pregnancy. We were relieved, both of us. But I think your father thought it was his fault. We couldn't eat as well as we should have. I was tired all the time. People can romanticize babies all they want, but babies take a lot of time and money. I was glad Willa didn't come for another two years. But your father, he can never do enough to deserve us. I don't think he ever forgave himself."

I wasn't convinced my father's pain over some unborn child was at the heart of his rage. But I understood her message. I helped her apply foundation around her bruised eye and decided I'd never have a baby. There was too much pain in the world already. Don't think I didn't imagine for a second what we could have had, you and me. But I couldn't dwell on it. You would never come back to me. And the pregnancy wasn't real except as a ticking time bomb, a group of cells that were multiplying over and over like a tumor in my body that I had to get rid of as soon as possible. I felt it at night, clawing its way, grabbing at everything around it and taking over my body.

54

It was Heather who told us about the apartheid protests. I was in the dining hall on Monday when Heather handed me a red flyer. "There's a meeting tonight," she said. I read: "Divest Now! Your Tuition Supports Apartheid in South Africa. Arts Quad, 8 PM. Be There!!!"

Heather and Daiyu were eager to go. Faye was curious. I hesitated at first, but I had no reason not to join them. I couldn't go back to my room alone. Panic stretched through me. It had started with the phone call to your house, and though it had loosened up after my conversation with Lloyd, since Lloyd hadn't arrived, it had become a taut wire in my chest that threatened to cut me in half.

I stood with my friends, and we cheered that night when a woman with a bullhorn stood on the steps leading to Theodore Weston's larger-than-life-size statue. I looked at the sky full of stars above us. There was talk about making the administration listen, and I listened. I heard them say that South Africa's racist policy was being supported by money from our school, our tuition, and that people of color were being denied basic human rights. Someone set off firecrackers, and I hit the ground so fast I bruised my elbows and knees. I heard Heather and Faye at my side asking if I was okay, but I couldn't get up just yet. Finally, Heather moved my arms away and looked at my face, and I realized how worried she was. I said I was fine, couldn't explain it, just startled. I saw them exchange looks.

They planned to build a living monument, a replica of the conditions people of color in South Africa had to live in. We were handed hammers and a bag of nails to build a house in a shantytown. The boy on the podium said we'd make a statement right here on our campus, since Weston College was investing in companies that did business with South Africa and therefore supporting the South African government.

"What if they arrest us?" I asked.

Heather shrugged. "We're not getting arrested right now," she said. "We're in a public space. No big deal."

"Are you sure?" I said.

"You don't have to stay if you don't want to," Faye said. "But my dad's a lawyer. He says they can't arrest all of us."

"I've got to look something up in the library, and then I'll come back," I told them.

"That's fine, leave us to do all the work," Heather joked.

I ended up meeting Serena for coffee. She was eager to share her exploits and ask me questions about love. I felt sorry for her that she didn't know when she was looking for it, because that's what I sensed behind her questions. She wanted love before she gave her life over to music. They didn't have to be mutually exclusive, did they? But she seemed to believe it could only be so. It had been three days since I'd spoken to Lloyd about you. Each night I picked up the phone, dialed his number, and hung up.

55

Faye had a boyfriend who was from Turkey. He was a philosophy major who talked about kismet. You would have called it unmyeong:

fate. I wondered how someone like you, who believed in fighting for your rights, could believe in something as passive as fate, as curses that couldn't be broken. How did you know?

56

Heather's face is still partially bloody from the first bullet that Lloyd fired in the room an hour ago. Only an hour, but it feels as if it's already been the entire day. Next is Daiyu, whose hair is still tangled, whose face has dried mud on it still, streaked with dirt and tears, and she's slumped forward—how much of the night was she held by crazy Lloyd? And then Faye, who sits with her back straight, but I can see the pinched expression in her cheeks, and I know she's scared for her life.

YOU DON'T THINK I'M SERIOUS. I'LL SHOW YOU SERIOUS.

I hold my breath.

Sax's voice comes through the receiver. "You're holding girls hostage in a college dorm with weapons, Lloyd. We're taking you seriously. Work with me here."

FUCK. CALL ME IN TWO MINUTES.

Lloyd sets the handset on the receiver. More gently than he's ever handled anything, and it scares me more than the violence.

Lloyd points the handgun at each of my friends in turn and finally lands on Heather. But then he picks the scissors off the floor and cuts the tape off her feet. She reaches down to rub her ankles with her bound hands.

Lloyd moves to Faye and cuts her feet apart too, and she sighs. I see him wince and hope he doesn't change his mind, but he steps back.

EENY, MEENY, MINY, MO. WHY SHOULD I LET YOU GO?

"Pick me, Lloyd. I have to go. We worked on the sit-in together, remember? It's tomorrow, remember all our plans? Daiyu's the one who lies all the time. She pretends to like everyone, but she—" Faye says. She's pushed herself to a standing position. "You can't let this derail the sit-in. Think about everything you did for it. And I know you believed in it, it's just like this Korea thing. If you let me out of here, I can—"

SIT-IN? YOU THINK I GIVE A SHIT ABOUT THAT? YOU AND ALL THE KIDS HERE WORKING TO END APARTHEID WHEN THE ONE WHO WOULD SAVE THE WORLD IS BEING TORTURED. YOU'RE OBLIVIOUS TO WHAT REALLY MATTERS. YOU'RE MANIPULATED BY WHATEVER THE MAINSTREAM PRESS TELLS YOU IS IMPORTANT. WHAT DO YOU CARE ABOUT APARTHEID? YOU'RE A RICH WHITE GIRL FROM CHICAGO. THE APARTHEID MOVEMENT WILL BE FINE WITHOUT YOU. YOU'RE THE MOST SELFISH PERSON I'VE EVER MET.

"I'm not selfish," Faye says.

There's silence, and Faye seems too close to Lloyd, and I'm afraid he'll swing at her or worse. He stares at her even though she's looking at the floor now, still standing but wavering. Heather must have sensed it too. She says, "Look, I never did anything to you."

Lloyd whirls toward her. He waves the gun in Daiyu's direction. BUT YOU DIDN'T HELP ME. DAIYU HELPED ME. Daiyu sits on the desk by the door.

"That's a lie. She was afraid of you," Faye says, re-energized, it seems.

"I wasn't." Daiyu stands.

"Faye, we were all afraid, but she did help him at first," Heather says. "All that time Yoona was sleeping with him."

"But I never . . ." I know I'm sputtering and can feel everyone's eyes on me, especially Lloyd's, and he looks at each of us in turn. I have to be careful here.

"I told you they were together," she continues.

"She told me she hated him. I was the one who told her to help him," Faye says, and she's sitting up again.

"We both told her to stay away, and if she'd listened to us, we wouldn't be here right now," Heather says.

"Stop it, stop fighting! Can you hear yourselves?" Daiyu shouts.

"We wouldn't be here if we'd never met Yoona," Faye says. There's silence as everyone looks at everything in the room but me.

"Lloyd, this is between you and me. Let all of them go. Sax will be so relieved, he'll give you whatever you want if you do that," I tell him. THAT'S A LIE.

"He'd be a hero, he'd think he's the best hostage negotiator around—just give him the girls, and I ll stay with you. I'll make sure we get what we want."

Lloyd taps the gun against his forehead. FUCK, FUCK, FUCK.

"We have to seem reasonable. Be diplomats. We can do it, but not with so many hostages in this room. It doesn't make us look good. Jaesung wouldn't want it this way."

He jumps to his feet, snatches the phone, and speaks into it. DETECTIVE? YOU THERE? I DON'T WANT TO SEE ANY OF YOUR MEN AT THE DOOR WHEN SHE GOES OUT. OR ELSE YOU'LL BE PICKING UP A BODY OUTSIDE THE DOOR. DO YOU HEAR ME?

I feel faint upon hearing his words. He's going to free one of them.

"We're working this out, Lloyd. Why would you think I'd try something like that? You still would have three girls inside after you release one. I'd be very bad at my job if I did something like that."

Lloyd nods as if it makes sense to him. LET PRESIDENT REAGAN KNOW I NEGOTIATED. I GAVE HIM ONE. I'M REASONABLE. He grabs Daiyu by the arm and pushes the gun into her back. GO. GET OUT OF HERE, BEFORE I CHANGE MY MIND.

Lloyd opens the door a crack and peers through, then goes back to Daiyu and holds on to her like a shield. She looks back at us, Heather, Faye, and me, sitting on the bed, farthest from the door.

GO AND TELL THEM I DIDN'T HURT ANY OF YOU. Lloyd pushes the gun into her back.

"We'll be okay, Daiyu," I call out to her.

She blinks and nods. Faye lets out a sob, and Heather shakes her head back and forth.

57

Serena walked with me to Intro to Asian Literature and then, in her usual manner, left me to sit by herself, aloof and alone. It was just the way she was. She didn't feel comfortable in crowds. It was not a huge lecture, but fifty was too large for her even though the auditorium could seat two hundred and fifty. I sat up front. Julian Wong was my favorite professor. But today I sat in class and heard nothing he said except for a poem by Hwang Chiu called "Even the Birds Are Leaving the World":

> A flock of white birds
> Leaving the field of reeds
> Fly in one, two, three files,
> Honking, giggling
> Carrying their own world,
> Separating their world from ours ·

I was sorry I was late again with an assignment, but I couldn't concentrate. I waited after class for Professor Wong and then walked with him, explaining I'd drop off my paper the next day. We were outside by then. He said he had a meeting across campus, but he listened. You would have liked him. Even when he was busy, he seemed interested. When more students joined us, clamoring for his attention, I moved aside. I picked up my pace and recommitted to writing that paper I owed him.

With all the students on campus spilling out to the quad between classes, I wouldn't ordinarily have noticed, but somehow that morning I did. A boy was standing in the middle of the walkway with a backpack on one shoulder, like so many students on campus, but something was different about him. He stood by the statue of the founder in the middle of quad, where the four paths converged. I made a move to cut across the grass, and out of the corner of my eye I saw that he'd taken steps too, off the grass, into my path. I knew right then that it was Lloyd.

He put down his backpack as if he had something breakable inside while keeping his eyes on me. I was in front of him in seconds, dropped my book bag on the ground at my feet, and we hugged each other. There was only one awkward moment, when he turned his face one way and I turned the same way, and he kissed me on the lips.

"I'm sorry it took so long to get here," Lloyd said. He looked the way I remembered him but with slightly puffier cheeks, as if he'd been crying or up all night. Dark circles under his eyes. He was wearing a green T-shirt and jeans. It was only September, but we'd already had frost that morning, and it was less than fifty degrees. I wondered if he was cold.

"What's this new look?" he said, apparently noticing what I was wearing too.

"What's wrong with it?" I said.

I pulled at the gray sweater that I wore over a white button-down shirt. Serena and I had found a secondhand store downtown last week and bought vintage men's shirts, long black skirts, and combat boots. A modernized interpretation of a hanbok.

"Jaesung wouldn't recognize you."

"I'm not so different," I said and ignored his stare. "What'd you find out?" I said and took his arm, steered him forward. The quad was emptying out. The next class period had started, but I couldn't think of going now that Lloyd was here. Across the quad by the library was the shantytown where Heather and Faye were working on their house. The sound of hammers pounding in nails carried across the quad.

"Are you okay?" he said.

"Talk to me. What's going on?" I said.

"It was terrible. I have nightmares about it." Closer now, I could see his face was wet with tears.

I put my arm around him, and he put his around me, and we walked, huddled together like that. "What happened?" I asked. "Take your time, I'm here."

"You've got to believe me," he said. "You're the only one who would believe me."

"Of course I believe you."

I felt hope bloom in my chest. It had been a little seedling, but now that Lloyd was here with me, I felt we would find you. Wherever you were, you weren't able to get back to us, but you were alive. As long as you were alive, I could wait. He returned my hug, and I thought, *We have to stick together, him and I.* Wherever it would lead. We'd find you. Me and your co-secretary of state or the one who would be secretary of state before you became one. You had trusted Lloyd. So I would too.

58

When Daiyu walks through that open doorway away from us, I hold my breath. Surely Detective Sax will use this opportunity to bust through and rescue all of us? I brace myself, and I nod at Heather and Faye to do the same. Even though Faye has said things to save herself, I will try to forgive her, even though it stings, even though neither she nor Heather look at me with anything but disgust.

Daiyu walks out and closes the door behind her, and we hear her steps fade down the hall.

"You'll go next," I whisper to Heather. She doesn't acknowledge me. Her head is turned toward the door. "You too." I lean back so I can see Faye, who is staring at the spot where Daiyu just stood. If Lloyd let her leave, then he'll let us too. This is going to be over soon—I feel it.

59

You and I loved the winds. The buses circled up and around on ribbons of roads beside the rice field–skirted mountains. At sporadic intervals, the tour guides would let us get off the bus and stretch our legs. Three busloads of American teenagers with our hair and shirts and skirts billowing out. The winds, cool enough to keep us from sweating, warm enough to prevent us from being chilled, wrapped us in tall gusts. The guides listed what we couldn't see hidden in the thick pine-, fir-, and oak-filled valley below us: wild boar, roe deer, musk deer, elk, gorals, black bears, yellow-throated martens, three kinds of weasels.

We stood behind waist-high stone walls and looked into a series of valleys, and even when the thermostat read 98 degrees Fahrenheit, the winds would blow so hard we could hardly hear the person who was beside us talking. There was a disturbance above us, and you pointed. In the sky, banking sharply in the air, wide ribbons of birds swooped and circled and then departed. I envied them their separateness from everything but themselves.

Someone asked what kind of birds they were, and a guide called out, "Orioles." Someone asked what kind, and another guide said we would call them black-naped orioles and then pointed into the valley. "Down there are special birds—cranes. Red-crowned cranes, white-naped cranes, hooded cranes," he said.

When Lloyd and the others went back to the bus, you and I stayed. You climbed up and looked out, then offered your hand to me. On top of that wall, it was as if we had stepped out into air and hovered with wings.

60

When Lloyd appeared on campus that first day, we walked and talked for hours. I made him repeat what he remembered about the last time he saw you. There was smoke. There were fire trucks. You and Lloyd were invited to a meeting by these students who drove you in separate cars, and on the way there was an accident. "But Jaesung's father said you were in the same car." I stopped him.

"That's a lie. I don't know why they told him that. We were separated, and Jaesung told me we should do what they said—meet up later. They were taking precautions in case they were followed."

"Who was following you?"

"Jaesung wanted to go with them. We agreed to whatever they said."

"And then?"

"It was only my car, Yoona. My car was in the accident."

"Your car caught on fire?"

"There wasn't a fire. That was what was weird." He paused and rubbed his eyes. "God, I'm tired," he said.

"We could go to my room. Do you need to lie down?"

"You know what, actually, I'm more hungry than tired. Could I eat first?"

I took him to the dining hall, and we found Heather, Daiyu, and Faye. They welcomed him with curious but warm smiles. "They've got chocolate chip," Heather said, holding out her cone to me.

Lloyd draped his arm around my neck. I squeezed his waist. No need to be nervous, I wanted to tell him. My friends made room for us at their table, but I didn't sit down right away.

"We should get some food," I said. "What's good?" I looked at my friends' trays. Remnants of mashed potatoes and roasted chicken were on one of them.

Daiyu stood up. "More cookies for me," she said and came over, hooking her arm through mine. I expected Lloyd to follow. "Oh god, he's cute," Daiyu whispered as we walked toward the entrée line. "You never said how cute he was."

We watched girls glance at him, and Daiyu giggled. I looked at Lloyd anew. I'd never thought of him that way. Without you taking the spotlight, maybe Lloyd was getting a chance to shine.

Lloyd didn't leave after dinner. Daiyu needed his help. Since I'd met her, she'd cut open the skin on her shin from falling down the stairs in the student union, sprained her thumb, and burned her arm with hot coffee. I've never seen anyone have so many accidents. She cut her hand on a piece of glass in the dining hall that evening, and Lloyd had Neosporin and bandages in his backpack. He patched her up like a medical professional. Daiyu was so grateful she invited him to a party in the student union, and he accepted. "Free beer is exactly what I need," he said. I wanted to talk to him some more about what had happened to you, but a few hours at a party wouldn't hurt. As we headed to the party, Lloyd talked to my friends, and I didn't say much. I was still mulling over what Lloyd had said about you earlier in the day. It didn't make sense, but what else did I have to hold on to?

As soon as we entered the large hall of the student union, Daiyu and Faye were called out to the dance floor by some friends. Heather and Lloyd went to see what beverages were available. I stood by myself. You and I had never gone dancing in Korea. The tour hadn't organized parties. Heather and Lloyd returned with large red plastic cups of beer and handed one to me. She said something to Lloyd, and he laughed, bobbing his body to the music pounding around us. Daiyu came dancing over to us and pulled Heather to the dance floor. I thought Lloyd had gone with them, but he was back with another cup of beer for me, and when I raised my cup to show him I still hadn't drunk mine, he downed both. "It's too loud," I told him.

"It's a party," he said as if I didn't understand this.

"Shouldn't you take it easy?" I said, indicating the empty beer cups in his hand.

He replied by nesting one in the other. "It's a party," he repeated. He started goofing off, dancing in place.

"Yeah, but aren't you tired?" I said.

"Don't want to think about anything right now, know what I mean?" he said.

I nodded, but I didn't entirely agree.

"Drink up." He nudged my cup to my lips. "Show me your moves," he said.

I reasoned if I did, we could get out of there sooner. The beer was surprisingly cold. When I looked back at Lloyd, he was fully involved in the music. "You've got me beat," I said, motioning to how he was dancing. He laughed at that, his head entirely thrown back. Just then Daiyu was back, and she synced her dance moves with Lloyd's. I didn't remember seeing Lloyd as relaxed and entertaining as he was now, flirting with Daiyu.

"Come on, let's go, dance, dance, dance," he said in my direction. After all he'd gone through, a night of dancing seemed to be a small respite.

I drank my beer and joined in. I don't know how long we were dancing. A few more beers replaced the one in my hand as Lloyd kept handing me full cups. Faye, Heather, and their friends joined us. Someone sloshed beer on my shirt, everyone oblivious. It snapped me back to reality. I looked at everyone dancing and laughing and drinking too much, and I had to get out of there. A wave of grief washed over me. Everyone was having fun meeting people, and I didn't want any of them, only you.

I left them dancing and drinking, the lights pulsing and the music throbbing. I walked out to a terrace beside the hall and then all the way to the railing and looked down at the waters of the gorge rushing below. What had happened to you? Your parents thought you were dead. How could they be so certain? But they were certain. I thought of your father's voice and of the fatigue in it. What else but a son's death could bring on that kind of crushing weight on every part of his being? But then there was Lloyd, who said you were still alive. You had to be alive. He was the last one who saw you.

In a trick of the moonlight and the shadows of the trees, I thought I saw someone standing below me, near the water's edge. Something about him made me think of you. It couldn't be. I knew it couldn't be. I tried to tell my legs to slow down. The stone steps were slippery in the dark, wet with leaves, but I went faster and faster. My heart was in my throat. But when I reached the bottom no one was there.

Lloyd found me sitting on the steps in tears. He sat next to me. "Kind of cold, don't you think?"

"Headache." I didn't wipe my eyes in the dark. He wouldn't know I'd been crying.

"I get those too. Migraines. They should rename them something that means 'shoot me now because it would feel better than this.'" He laughed at his cleverness.

I let out a half laugh to join him.

He edged closer to me. "I think I drank too much."

"Probably."

"Your friends are nice. Daiyu and Heather and Faith."

"Faye. Her name is Faye, not Faith."

"Right, Faye."

"I need you to tell me more about that last day with him."

"He told me once, I guess it was on the tour, he said you guys were alike. You wanted to be in the service of other people, life goals, you know. He said, If you want Yoona to do something, tell her someone else will be hurt if she doesn't do it."

"What? You're making that up. He never said that."

"Maybe I'm drunk."

"You're definitely drunk. Weird thing to say."

"I can't stop thinking about him."

Hearing him admit that made it impossible for me to hold back. I hung my head in my folded arms and sobbed. He put an arm around me, and in that cold air, the warmth was welcome.

"Where is he, Lloyd?" I wept.

He was mumbling. "I asked Jaesung once what he saw in you. He said you had sequins. I said what kind. He said sparkly ones. Do you? Do you have sparkly sequins?"

"You're making no sense," I said.

"I told him it was lust, pure lust." He chuckled.

"I prefer that version," I said.

"Me too. Lust is better."

"Not sure it's better, Lloyd." I had to laugh. He laughed too.

"It's nice here. There's been no nice place since the fire."

"So the car did catch on fire?"

"No, no, no, the firemen wouldn't be there if there weren't a fire."

"Right. So there was a fire." I felt tears well up again.

"Only smoke. You've got to believe me. He needs us, Yoona."

I huddled closer to him. "I believe you, Lloyd. I believe you, and you know what? Jaesung said you were the smartest guy he knew."

"He said that about me?"

"Yeah."

Lloyd turned his cup of beer over, but nothing was left in it to spill out. We sat in silence for a while, and then he said, "Now I've got a headache. You tricked me, Yoona."

"I'm sorry, Lloyd."

"Sequins."

I made him get to his feet, and we went back to my room to sleep off whatever we both were filled with.

61

"I'll find you." Your words. How certain you sounded. We make such promises as if we know the future. And we count on them as if words have power.

62

I could think of nothing but how to find you. I proposed to Lloyd that we scour microfiche of Korean newspapers for anything that mentioned the accident in August, to research eyewitness accounts of secret service operatives in Asia. I insisted we read everything we could get our hands on, searching for any hints of what might have happened on August 21 in Seoul. The American newspapers only focused on preparations for the winter Olympics. I grilled Lloyd again and again on that night in Seoul. I drafted letters to your parents and planned what Lloyd might say to them and then what I'd say. "If we have proof, they will believe us," I said.

It was my idea to call the hospital in Korea where Lloyd said he'd been taken on the night of the accident. I planned to ask for his records and that of anyone else who had been involved. If your parents were told you'd died that night, there would be a report, wouldn't there? The problem was we didn't have any money to call Korea.

I called my mother and asked her if she could ask my aunt to call me. I explained about you, though I called you a friend only, and how there had been an accident and now this confusion about your whereabouts.

"Your aunt is traveling with your uncle on business," she told me.

"Well, when will she be back?"

"How are your classes, Yoona?"

"I need to talk to her. How can I talk to her?" I said.

"I wish you'd never gone to Korea this summer."

"What does that mean?"

"Who was this boy to you?"

I couldn't tell her, not after what Willa had gone through with her boyfriend, and I could hear suspicion in her voice. I knew what she'd say: *You're just like your sister, ruining yourself over a boy.* I told her to send me more money for school supplies and hung up. Just before I'd gone to Korea for the summer, my sister, Willa, had left school with her boyfriend to join a religious cult in Arizona. It's what made my parents agree to send me to Korea. And now, six months later, Willa was back in Lakeburg. Her boyfriend had fallen in love with another woman, and my sister had realized her mistake in giving up her education for a man. Were broken hearts inevitable in our family?

Lloyd and I had an uncanny connection during this time. Lloyd called it being on the same wavelength. He'd appear wherever I was, wandering into the same room I was in at the library or finding me in line at the bookstore. Even though he didn't have a key to my room, we never had to plan when we'd meet—he'd just find me or I'd see him walking by on campus. We each seemed to know where the other person was. We were tuned in to each other.

Late at night, Lloyd and I went over the possibilities. Late into the night, huddled together in my bed, under the covers, reassuring ourselves, planning what could have happened to you. We fit on my narrow twin bed. There were no misunderstandings about what we meant to each other. We were pals, cohorts. I insisted on my being in love with you. He said he knew. When he asked me about a boy I was talking to on campus, outside a class. I explained we were assigned a project together, and he said you might be jealous. I understood he was protective of me for your sake. This was what best friends did for each other. We had a mission to find you, and he was my partner in it. He didn't appear to be uncomfortable in the least. I teased him about Daiyu when he mentioned her name. We were the same, Lloyd and I.

"It could be amnesia—that's what he has. He might be alive in Korea right now, living in some small town. Someone could have taken his wallet, or he could have given it to someone, and then that person was in an accident and the police thought it was him—and they reached his parents. He was always giving money and stuff away. You know he was," I began.

"And it could have been a fire. These cars catch fire all the time," Lloyd said.

"Or he could be sick in a hospital somewhere, not able to tell anyone. Maybe he's in a coma."

"Yeah, I can see that. Or the KCIA is torturing him somewhere."

"No." I shook my head. I didn't want to imagine that.

"He was with those student organizers. They don't know he's American, that's it, and—because those cars looked pretty official, Yoona. That's the part that makes me nervous. They didn't look like regular students. I warned Jaesung about them."

"Maybe it's North Korea—there were those kidnappings, remember? Remember the guys at the other table in the mandu shop? They said they kidnapped fishermen, remember?"

"But how could they move around so easily in South Korea? These were official vehicles, Yoona. The fire trucks came as if they knew what was going to happen before it did."

"But you said there wasn't a fire?"

"No, but the fire trucks came as if there had been one. I saw them. You said you believed me. No one believes me, but I'm telling you, they were there, which I thought was weird. And then I woke up in the hospital, and no one would tell me what had happened. You believe me, don't you?"

"I do, I do believe you, shh . . ." I held him close to me. "You're the only one who can help him now."

"Me and you," Lloyd said.

"Yes." And I stroked his hair and listened to his breathing quiet as he fell asleep. I didn't tell him what was nagging at me, the tiny thought that circled around and around in my head. Had you found a way to set yourself on fire and jump with those students after all? Is that why you and Lloyd were in separate cars? Is that why your parents were so certain you were gone? I pushed it out of my head. You'd promised me you'd find me. You'd find me in the States. You didn't talk about martyrs by the end of the tour. You'd changed. I knew you'd changed your mind about it.

"Where've you been?" Serena said the next time I saw her walking to class, the day after Lloyd showed up.

"So much has happened," I said.

"Daiyu said you were with some boy," she said. "Cute boy."

"He was the last to see Jaesung."

I could tell Serena wanted to tell me about her night, but I knew I was running out of time.

"How do you talk to your dad in Korea?" I asked.

"He calls me, why?"

"I need to get some information."

"About Jaesung?"

"We need to confirm the body was actually his. Hospital records, to start."

"You said his parents identified the body."

"I have to be sure."

"Do you hear yourself?"

"I have to call people in Korea who can look into it. Like Tongsu Cho. He's a friend of Jaesung's. He set up the meeting that night of the accident."

"Look, if I have to reach my dad, if it's an emergency, I go to Dean Olin's office and use his phone. His phone can make international calls."

"What about the time difference?"

"Doesn't matter. If it's an emergency, I wake my dad up."

"Olin is in the finance building?"

"Underwood, yeah. Second floor. Name is on the door."

Serena didn't think much of my friends Heather, Daiyu, and Faye. But she didn't like groups either, so I didn't think much of it. I'd see her in the dining hall, and she'd walk away as if we'd never met. I told her she had to work on being more social if she wanted the whole college experience she claimed she did. Heather, Daiyu, and Faye stayed away from Serena, but Lloyd walked right up to her and didn't understand when she walked away as if she hadn't heard him announce to her who he was.

"That's Lloyd, the one Daiyu told you about—he's a friend of Jaesung," I said when I saw her at the student union as we watched Lloyd study a bulletin board of announcements.

"Something's weird about him," she said, wrinkling her nose as if she smelled something unpleasant.

"Because he talked to you?"

"What is he to you exactly?"

"He's the only person I know who knew Jaesung as well as I did."

"He doesn't act like he's your friend."

"So now you're an expert on friendships? After what—three weeks of having friends?"

"I saw him carrying you out of the Tap Room, Yoona. You were drunk."

"So what? I was drunk, and he was carrying me back to my room. What are you saying?"

"Yeah, you were drunk." She made a face and left me.

The thing was I remembered drinking sometimes with him when we had one of our sessions, brainstorming what could have happened to you. We'd be walking, and suddenly he'd pull me into a doorway and say he had to tell me a breakthrough idea. Sometimes he'd pull me into the Tap Room, and we'd sit in the corner drinking so we could come up with a plan. I could never handle drinking much without feeling dizzy. I'd wake hours later in bed with him, my shoes still on my feet.

Lloyd and I were running out of ideas.

One night the crowd in the dining hall was thinning out. Lloyd came to dinner late and threw a flyer on the table. "Korea Society meetings start tonight," he said, looking around at us for a response.

"Do you think they'll have food?" Heather said. "I hear the Chinese Student Association has great food."

"Oh my god, you think?" Daiyu giggled. "So much better than this junk." She pushed her plate of salad away.

"CSA is meeting tonight at the same time. Bummer," Faye said.

"Let's go to both. Chinese Student Association and Korea Society. My father is Korean and my mother is Chinese," Daiyu said. "Technically, I could go to both. Are you going?" she said to Lloyd.

Lloyd didn't seem to hear her and snatched the flyer. "Yoona, let's go. I don't care what the rest of you do." Then he left the dining hall.

We looked at each other in surprise. "Whoa," Heather said.

"I better find out what's going on," I said.

"When he yells at us like that? How long is he going to be around?" Faye asked. "Isn't he at Harvard or something?"

"Columbia," Daiyu corrected.

I felt my face redden as they turned to me as if I'd be able to explain Lloyd's behavior. They had the look my sister and I gave my mother at these moments. I knew it well.

Just then I saw Serena heading toward the door. "I've got to go," I said and picked up my tray and backpack. It had been a few days since I'd seen her.

I asked her if she was going to the Korea Society meeting. She shook her head. "I'd never go to those things. They're exclusive."

"What happened to your experiencing-everything-about-life project?"

"Whatever. Anyway, I can meet you tomorrow for coffee again. It's been a nightmare these three days. My father insists I go to New York to have some dumb radio interview with a Korean radio station. I told him I'm a student here, and I can't miss my classes. He's promised I can do it over fall break, but only because I talked to him every single day and made him understand it was absolutely impossible for me to leave campus right now."

"A radio station in Korea?"

"For when I go to Korea. They've got a partnership with the BBC, so they're using their station, but the interviewer is from the Korean station—I don't know. Plus a *New York Times* reporter wants to talk to me."

"Radio would be perfect. They're from Korea?"

"Why are you so interested in radio? Aren't you a comp lit major?"

"Do you think the Korean person from the radio station would talk to me? If you can get a number? I could call and get more information about Jaesung."

She nodded. "Right, okay, but speak to them yourself. I'll tell my dad three first-class tickets."

"Why three? Is he coming here to fly over with us?"

"For Aloe Moon. He flies right next to me. He's never seen the inside of a baggage compartment. Horrors!" she said. She'd told me already that her cello was named Aloe Moon.

We parted ways at the fork in the walkway. I was walking in the direction I'd seen Lloyd go, toward the student union where the Korea Society meeting would be held, when Lloyd jumped out at me and grabbed my arm. He began walking rapidly back the way we'd come, pulling me along. I pulled back. "What're you doing? We—the meeting is the other way," I said. He pulled me closer and whispered, "That girl you were talking to, I know her from somewhere."

"You met her before. That's Serena Im."

"Was she on the tour with us? I swear she might have been. I know I know her from somewhere." Lloyd was sweating even though it wasn't hot outside. His forehead glistened with perspiration.

"You're mixing her up with someone else. I do that too. Come on, we're going to be late for the meeting. You okay?"

He nodded and released me. He seemed deflated. "Just tired. Yeah, let's go. Of course, come on."

I rubbed his shoulders, patted his back. "Hey, I've got good news. Serena's dad has ties to the *Times* and NPR and Korean media too. I'm going to ask her to help us."

"Don't." He stopped short as he spoke, and tension returned to his face.

"We need to talk to the right people, Lloyd. Someone who might know about the fire trucks going out to the site of the accident, someone who has access. Journalists could have that access."

"Not through her."

"Why?" His response was frustrating me.

"She's not telling you everything. Don't trust her."

"What? Serena's a little odd, and she didn't talk to you, I get that, but she's the only one who can help us."

"It's not because she didn't talk to me. Come on, I have a feeling about these things."

"A feeling?"

"You don't believe me."

"Come on, Lloyd." I put my bag on the ground and made him look at me, my hands on his arms in front of him. "Look, it's not her we have to trust. We need a journalist who has access in Korea, in Seoul."

"I think this Korea Society meeting will be safer."

"How?"

"Don't look at me like that. Yoona? Come on, let's see what they say at this meeting. You're blinded by Serena. I don't know why, but she has a hold on you."

"You're kidding me, right?"

"Daiyu is your real friend. Serena isn't who you think she is."

I didn't understand, but I picked up my bag and tried to put the whole conversation out of my mind. I put my arm through his. "Okay, I'll go with you. Come on, we're going to be late. Let's go."

The meeting was on the second floor of the student union. Someone was speaking. We walked between clumps of people standing around and saw Faye and Daiyu waving to us.

"A lot of exciting new events this year," a stocky boy in a polo shirt was saying into a microphone in the back of the room. "My name is Thomas Bang, and you elected me president last year. Welcome. I'm happy to see new faces here. Be sure to sign your name on the sheet where you came in so we know how to reach you to let you know about upcoming events. One of them next month is the barbecue on the south lawn, so if you have a good time here tonight, we hope you'll join us on October fifteenth. There's a calendar up front too—and you can ask me or John Koh. Where are you, John?"

I joined everyone in clapping for him. Then John Koh, a boy up front, waved the sign-in sheet and said something about how great Thomas Bang was, and Thomas Bang waved in acknowledgment, and we all clapped again. "I've seen him before," Lloyd said. I looked around the room. "He was on the tour," Lloyd whispered to me. I had to admit this time Lloyd was right. John had been on our bus. Our eyes met, John's and mine, and he raised a hand in our direction. I raised a hand back in greeting.

"Small world," I said.

"Too small," Lloyd answered.

"But this could be a good thing," I said. "Maybe he knows something."

"Doubt it," Lloyd replied.

"Why are you so negative all of a sudden?"

"I'm just tired. I should go back to the city. I don't know what I'm doing here."

"But you can't give up now. Lloyd, you were there. You saw him in the other car. Someone here, maybe John, can help us."

Lloyd turned away from me as Thomas began speaking again about events they hoped to hold during the year. He talked about more sign-up sheets, babysitting that grad students with families needed, and field trips to local wineries. They needed tutors too, to help the Korean grad students. "You could learn Korean, some of you could improve your Korean, and you could help them with English," he said. And then he talked about ways to raise money for the Olympic athletes.

"What about organizing around politics, like they're doing for the antiapartheid protests in South Africa?" Lloyd cupped his hands and shouted.

Heads turned in our direction. People stared. I whispered low at him, "Let's talk to him privately."

Lloyd turned away from me and held his fingers to his lips as people coughed uncomfortably, cleared their throats.

"Always drama at the Korea Society, am I right?" Thomas said, and everyone laughed. "Thanks to Youn Lim for organizing tonight's meeting. And over there is Z-MC, providing us with great music," Thomas continued, giving a single wag of his finger over his head. And with that, a boy with large headphones at a record player and speakers in the far corner raised one hand to everyone and started to spin some tunes with his other.

"Come on." Lloyd took my arm and pulled me out of the crowd toward the door. He had a scowl on his face and was wiping his nose with the back of his hand.

"Where are you going?" I said.

"There's nothing here but a party," Lloyd said and kept walking, pulling me along, refusing to let me go. It was the first time I felt helpless against him. Outside, he released me and kicked the base of a sculpture. We stood under a spotlight. Students walked past us.

"Don't ever do that to me again," I said and held my arm where he'd grabbed me.

He rushed over and put his arms around me. "I'm sorry, I'm sorry, I know. That was wrong. I know. I've got to get out of here. If I don't, I'm going to do something I regret, I know I will. It's the accident. It's made me like this. I don't want to be like this. Yoona, say you forgive me. Please. Say it. Please?"

I looked into his face. I knew what he was feeling, I told myself. I felt it too—the helplessness and despair. We were no closer to finding you than we had been two weeks ago. This place, this campus where life wasn't quite real life but something like a circus. Something false. And you were out there suffering. What, I didn't want to imagine.

"You can call Korea from your house phone if you go back to New York," I said.

"My mom gave me hell over the phone bill last time, but if she kicks me out again, I'll just come back here." He shrugged.

"Your mom kicked you out?"

"That's why I came here. I was calling Korea constantly, trying to find Tongsu Cho, and I was close too. I had to know, you know?"

"Did she really kick you out? Like, where would you have gone if you couldn't come here?"

"I've got a car, so no big deal." He gave me a small smile.

113

"She's awful."

"Yeah, well, my stepmother, you know, fits the stepmother stereotype. There's always one, you know."

"Well, come back here if she does that, promise?"

"That's a promise, and then I'll fall apart again."

"I feel it too, like there's nothing we can do, but we have to do something."

He nodded. "I'll try to call Korea again when I get home. I'll be in touch. Go study."

"I can't."

"Go, I'll let you know as soon as I find anything."

"Promise?"

"You bet."

He reached over and gave me a hug, and I squeezed him back and turned so he wouldn't see that I was on the verge of crying. He was abandoning us, you and me.

That night on campus after the Korea Society meeting, Lloyd got back into his little red car and promised to call. And even though I felt we'd failed you, I let him go.

63

You used to say we make our own luck. But you believed in curses too.

64

No one comes through that door after Daiyu leaves. I can feel Heather's and Faye's nervousness increase. Staring at the door isn't going to make it open for them. Lloyd stands at the window, the handgun's muzzle holding back the curtain, allowing a sliver of light to fall on the floor, a fraction of a view for him of the parking lot.

"Can you see Daiyu?" I call over to him.

HE FUCKING LIED TO ME.

I try to stay calm even though Lloyd still sounds angry. He let Daiyu go. That means something. He's going to let us all go soon. He has to. "Who do you mean?" I ask as if we're talking about someone he's read about in the news.

He answers, IT'S A TRICK. He's still studying what's happening outside, but this is a conversation I can work with. There are sounds of men shouting and applause. TWO MEN ON EACH SIDE OF HER WHEN SHE WALKED OUT OF THE BUILDING. HE SAID NO ONE WAS IN THE BUILDING.

"He said no one was in the hallway," I said.

YOU'RE LYING.

"I heard it too. You said hall, and he said hall," Faye says.

"Me too," Heather adds, but her face is still turned to the door.

"You're being paranoid, Lloyd. Maybe I should tell Sax to hurry up with the car. I'll have to go to the bathroom soon," I say.

Lloyd releases the curtain and turns to me. GO AHEAD, CALL.

"With my hands like this?" I make an effort to laugh at the ridiculousness of my predicament.

STOP LAUGHING AT ME.

"Laughing? I'm not laughing at you. Lloyd, I was just talking about my hands being—"

He grabs the phone and thrusts it up to my face. TALK.

"You won't show me the proof you have. You say you care about this baby—"

TALK.

"Tape is too tight. How will I have this baby you say you care about if I lose circulation in my hands?"

FINE.

Instead of putting the receiver back on the phone, he leaves it on the bed beside me, picks up the scissors again, and opens the blades. HOLD STILL. I can't quite believe what I'm seeing.

Faye nods as if she can hurry him up by moving her jaw up and down, and she even smiles a cramped smile. "Me too," she says. "My hands hurt too." As he slices through the tape around my wrists, part of it sticks, and he jerks the blades up. I keep it taut by keeping my wrists low. The tip of the scissors clips the inside of my wrist, and I react with a shout louder than I intended.

He drops the scissors as I pull my hands free and rub the cut. It's not even bleeding, but it stings. WHY DID YOU MOVE? ARE YOU OKAY?

I jerk away from his hands, which are all over my wrists and my waist, patting me as if to make sure I exist. I respond by recoiling from his hands, and then I stop because he's stopped and dropped his hands to his sides and is studying me with suspicion. It seeps out of his clenched hands.

65

After the Korea Society meeting, Lloyd and I said good-bye. I went back to my dorm, which felt empty without him now. My mother called. I told her I was studying. She wanted details, but I told her I was busy. My aunt was still away. I wasn't interested in anything else she had to say. When she asked, I told her about my classes. The lies were piling up, but I couldn't quit school as my sister had. My mother sounded as if my success in school cheered her up. She said, "I'm so proud of you, Yoona. I think about how hard you're studying, and it makes my day better. I can't describe how, but it just does."

I called John Koh, but though he remembered me from the tour, he didn't know anything about the car accident outside Seoul that had killed you and hurt Lloyd. He said he had returned to the United States the day after the tour ended. Instead of going to my classes, I went to the library and read accounts of what was happening in Korea. A librarian in the tech center handed me microfiche and said that someday soon we could go to a computer and read the news, the very latest news, with no delay. She called it the "Internet," and she showed me how to send an e-mail to someone on the other side of the world. But I didn't know anyone who knew about e-mail in Korea.

Serena found me in the library that afternoon.

"Did Lloyd break up with you or something?" she said.

"He was never my boyfriend," I answered without looking up.

"Did you forget that Aloe Moon and I are going to New York, and you're coming with us? A car is coming to take us to the airport in an hour. Hurry up."

I'd forgotten about it after Lloyd had dismissed the idea, but I didn't admit it. But now it came back—the possibility that I could talk to a journalist who could help me find you. I promised to meet her in her room and went off to pack a bag.

In New York, Serena, her cello, and I were driven in a limousine to a tall building in midtown. A pair of interns, a young woman and a young man, met us at the entrance, got us cleared by security in the lobby, and escorted us to the seventh floor. Serena and Aloe Moon disappeared into a studio, and the male intern led me to a room with a large window so I could see them perform and then talk to a man with a headset on. They gave Serena headphones too. She was in a room that had thick wires hanging in coils from the ceiling and large microphones suspended from the wires. The room I was in had men at sloped desks with levers and buttons. The intern told me to take a seat in the back and then sat next to me. We could hear Serena and the radio personality chatting it up. I was impressed by how comfortable she sounded, how smoothly she answered his questions about her life. Everyone was Korean and they spoke in Korean. I asked the intern in Korean how much contact they had with their counterparts in Seoul. He looked surprised. "All the time. Our listeners are in Korea."

"Would you know who I could speak to about getting news from Korea? I need to find out about a car accident that took place outside of Seoul in August."

The intern studied me warily—he seemed prepared to work with Serena's people, but he looked as if he was starting to realize my presence was unrelated.

"Who are you again?"

"It doesn't matter. A friend was in an accident, I just want more information about it. I was here, and it was in Korea, so I don't know how to find out what happened exactly."

"System isn't digital yet. When it is, it will be easy to access stuff like that."

"August twenty-first, eight p.m., Seoul. Large explosion, car fire. Whether it happened the way I heard it did or not, I need the official report, and maybe if there was media coverage, or maybe if someone like a journalist could investigate it for us."

A woman with a walkie-talkie in her hand came over to him and whispered something in his ear. He got up without a word to me and returned with a cup of coffee, which he handed to her. He didn't sit back down next to me, but instead moved over to the other intern, who was writing in a notebook. There wasn't much space in that engineering room, and it was dark. I waited to talk to him again, but then the interview was over, and a woman ushered me out, and I was left standing in the hallway. It wasn't much longer before Serena was released from her obligations and found me. She took one look at my face and asked me what was wrong. I told her about you and the intern's words.

"He's only an intern. What does he know?" she said.

"But what if Lloyd's right? What if Jaesung is alive?"

"He's dead, Yoona. You're seriously dreaming if you won't accept it."
Serena gave me such a pitying look I regretted saying as much as I had.

"Forget it," I said.

She wrinkled her nose as if she were about to sneeze, but then
didn't. "Listen, we're going to miss our flight. Come on, something is
weird about your friend Lloyd. Something's wrong with him."

"You just don't like him," I said as she turned and pressed the elevator button. I didn't offer to help her maneuver Aloe Moon even as she
held him out toward me.

"Monica Aronsteen had a stalker who had the same look in his eye.
She had to get an order of protection against him. He used to sit way in
the last row of the concert hall and just watch for hours." She shuddered.

"Lloyd isn't like that."

"Whatever. Look, I'll ask my father to look into it. He went to
school with someone at the *Chosun Ilbo*. He'd do anything for my dad,"
she said matter-of-factly. "I'm sorry about your friend. You should have
asked me."

"But I did. I did ask you," I said.

"No, you asked about how I called Korea."

I couldn't tell her she was wrong or that she didn't listen well, or
how I didn't know what to think. She was right, but I didn't trust her
to remember to ask her father. She was already talking about frozen hot
chocolate at some restaurant near Bloomingdale's. I followed her into
the elevator when it arrived.

"Come on," she said. "You can't mourn Jaesung forever. The sooner
you accept it, the better."

At the airport we were early to the boarding gate, and I left Serena
without telling her where I was going. I called Lloyd on a pay phone

across the hall. I could still see Serena, and she looked at me curiously. A woman answered and made me wait awhile before I heard Lloyd's voice. "I knew it was you. Had a feeling. What do you mean you're in New York?" he said.

"We're on the same wavelength again. I'm here! Well, I'm at JFK, but I came here with Serena for her interview. Who was that? Have you found Tongsu Cho?"

"My mom—she answers all calls and takes the phone with her when she leaves. Can you believe it? Wait, JFK? I'll come get you."

"Flight's boarding soon. Tell me about Tongsu Cho."

"It's useless."

"Don't say that. Did you call?"

"Can't believe my dad is going along with her. They control everything. You should see the look on her face when she told me I had a phone call." He laughed. "She's listening in right now, I bet."

"So buy another phone and plug it in when they're gone."

"Hah! Don't say that too loud. She'd love that. That way, they'll never give me back my passport, and this time when they kick me out, it'll be for good. What's going on at school? How are you?"

"What happened to your passport?"

"Yeah, that one's my dad's idea. He thinks I'll try to run away to Korea. With what money, I don't know what he thinks. I did take his credit card a few times, so maybe he has reason to doubt me. I thought about sending a telegram to the tour to ask about Tongsu. You sound different, how come?"

"That's good—try that. How different? Do you know where he keeps the passport?"

"In the safe in the store. You sound really close. I'm sorry I haven't called. Are you mad? I promise I'm working on finding Jaesung. It's all I think about. The phone situation sucks. Hey, we have to fly to North Dakota and convince them there's something wrong with the story they were told," Lloyd said.

"They won't believe us." I remembered your uncle's voice. "We don't have any evidence."

"I can explain, if they give me a chance, face to face. They'll believe me."

"I believed you."

"Exactly. Let me pick you up. We should have thought of this earlier, and you could have come back with me."

"We've got to convince Jaesung's parents he's alive." I saw Serena wave to me near the gate. "I've got to go," I said.

"We're running out of time," Lloyd said.

I hung up and hurried to board the plane.

66

YOU CAN'T STAND ME.

I have to tell the truth. I remember my mother knew this when my father raged. I stammer, "It's this whole thing, this thing you're doing right here, Lloyd. I was wrong not to tell you about the pregnancy. Honestly, I still can't accept that it's real. It's not real to me, do you understand? The whole thing, my body, everything about me right now, the way you touched me—if anyone touches me, it makes my skin crawl."

BUT IT'S JAESUNG'S BABY. YOU SAID YOU LOVE HIM. DOESN'T IT MEAN ANYTHING TO YOU? DON'T YOU LOVE ANYONE BUT YOURSELF?

"I did, but when I heard—look, you don't know what it's like. I feel like my body has been taken over. It's not mine, but it is mine, and I want it back. I'm eighteen, Lloyd."

BUT YOU'RE THE MOTHER OF HIS CHILD. There's a plaintive tone to his voice. I would have thought this once, idealized it, maybe, but not now.

The phone rings, and Lloyd answers it, turning his back to me. Heather inches forward, and the mattress creaks, but Lloyd doesn't notice. He's busy listening to whoever is on the phone, and holds it close to his ear so we can't hear.

No. He slams the phone back into its cradle and spins around to us. Heather slumps, returning to her position. Faye moves her shoulder in front of Heather's shoulder as if to keep her in place.

Lloyd rubs the side of the gun against his forehead like a washcloth and looks at me. A glimpse of my old friend Lloyd is in his eyes. I appeal to it.

"I don't want to be anyone's mother."

SO WHAT? WHY DOES IT MATTER WHAT YOU WANT? He hits his face with the gun. He seems to be fighting a part of himself.

I hold out my hand to him. "Lloyd, let's talk about this without the police outside, without Faye and Heather. We'll figure out what to do. We'll go home. You'll come with me to Lakeburg, and we'll figure out what to do. If you want me to keep the baby, we'll talk about it."

YOU'RE LYING.

"I'm serious. I'm sorry, I see now why you had to bring Daiyu here, you had to get Heather and Faye in here, to get me to listen to you. I see you had no choice."

YOU DIDN'T GIVE ME A CHOICE. YOU SAID YOU WERE GOING HOME TO YOUR PARENTS' HOUSE. YOU SAID THAT TO ME, DIDN'T YOU, IN THE QUAD? YOU SAID, 'LLOYD, I'M NOT GOING TO THE CLINIC, I'M GOING TO LAKEBURG.'

His voice has taken on a screech as if he's in pain. I WAS ALL ALONE. I DID WHAT I HAD TO DO.

67

On the plane with Serena that day, flying back to Weston from New York, I regretted not taking a chance and driving with Lloyd to your house in North Dakota. I should have let him pick me up and gone with him. We should have at least tried. And if that didn't work, we'd figure out something in New York. I had no further plans beyond something as vague as that, but I still regretted not trying. We'd figure it out. Me and Lloyd. As simple and as thoughtless as that. Silly girl. But part of me knew we didn't have the money or the plan.

I listened to Serena talk on and on about where she was going to tour, and I finally snapped at her, "Why are you at Weston? You sound like you should be doing what your dad says instead of pretending to be a college student." She didn't reply, just stared at me for a few seconds and then turned to the window.

What was I doing with her? Playing her sidekick as she played around with things that didn't matter. How did her music matter in the face of what had happened to you? Why wouldn't she help me find you?

I called Lloyd when I returned to my dorm, and this time the phone rang and rang and rang, and I pictured the empty phone socket, the cord wrapped around the body of the phone in his mother's purse somewhere—wherever she was. Lloyd was a prisoner in his own house. When the phone rang back in my room a few minutes later, I thought it was him, that we were on the same wavelength, as he said, but it was my mother asking me where I'd been. I explained about Serena. "You didn't tell me you were going to New York," she said, panic in her voice. "Where else are you going without telling me? Just like Willa. You're supposed to be studying."

"It was interesting, the radio station." I tried to spin it the way she might appreciate it. "Serena is a famous musician. She'll tour Korea. Ask your sister about her."

"Are you planning to go back to Korea? There have been more protests—it's not a safe place, Yoona. Your father won't allow it."

"No, why would you think Korea?"

"You've only been talking about going back there."

"Maybe I need to go to North Dakota."

"Why? What's in North Dakota? Are you quitting school to join a commune like your sister?"

"I'll call you tomorrow," I said and hung up the phone, and then I didn't go to my classes. Instead I holed up in the library, combing through Korean newspapers, looking for evidence. And I stopped at the job board. Maybe I could make enough money for Lloyd and me to buy our own tickets to North Dakota.

68

LOVE, LOVE, LOVE. ALL I'VE EVER GIVEN YOU WAS LOVE. His pacing is leading him farther and farther away from the shotgun. If he puts the handgun down, we could have a chance.

He whirls and charges me. EVERYTHING WE'VE BEEN THROUGH AND YOU'RE STILL LYING TO ME, YOONA.

69

In the middle of the night, there was a knock on my door, and I opened it to find Lloyd on the other side. "She wouldn't let me call you," he said and pushed past me into the room. "I scraped enough money together for gas, but the bridge tolls are going to mail a bill to the house. I didn't know how that was going to work. I thought they'd stop me." He paced back and forth, looking at the floor, his hands in his hair.

"Okay, it's okay." I closed the door and urged him to sit on the bed. "Lloyd, you're all right. You're here."

"I remembered something." He sat beside me, his arm around me, and whispered as if someone could hear us. "Tongsu Cho works at a restaurant called Little Pan in Itaewon. We can reach him there."

I leaned back and spoke in a normal volume. "What happened to your face?"

He had a scratch on his cheek that he traced now with his finger. It hadn't scabbed over yet. He leaned forward, still talking in a whisper. "She kicked me out."

"Did she do that to you?"

"This? No, it's from something else. But I found the number for the restaurant." He fished in his pocket, standing up to reach deep, and came up with a scrap of paper that he unfolded to show me a number starting with a Korean area code. He handed it to me, sitting back down.

"We can call from Underwood, the finance building. That's how Serena calls her dad."

"Let's go." He looked at his watch. "It's five p.m. in Seoul. The restaurant will be open."

I took out a pair of jeans and turned away from him before I climbed into them.

"You don't have to be shy with me," he said.

"What did you say?"

"Oh shit, that came out wrong. I meant, Hey, we've got to figure out how to call this number."

I finished buttoning up my jeans and pulled a sweater over my head with my back still turned to him. "I don't know how we can get into Dean Olin's office. There's a larger office where the secretaries sit and then the counter where they handle students who stop by. Outside of that is a larger door."

"I've opened locked doors before."

"How do you learn something like that?"

"Two stores down from my dad's shop is Mr. Kelly's locksmith shop. Mr. Kelly liked me hanging around, so he showed me a few things. But Mr. Kelly sold my dad the safe in his shop, so I can't open that one. I mean, I tried, but he made sure I couldn't open that one. Fuck Mr. Kelly."

I buttoned my coat and then held up my dorm room key. "Could you open the lock on my door?"

"Probably, maybe, but I never tried. I wouldn't. Plus you've got a dead bolt."

"Right. Anyway, you don't need to."

"Exactly, so there you go."

"So you can unlock most doors?"

"We'll see—is Underwood the brownstone one with the green door?"

"Near the main gate."

"Thought so. Let's go." He held the door open for me.

"Do you need any tools or anything?" I said as I turned out the light.

"We'll stop at my car."

"Good thing your parents didn't take that away."

"My mom couldn't get rid of me then. She'd rather I drive far away. Probably get in a car accident so she never has to see me again."

"You don't mean that."

"It's that or having me locked up."

We walked down the steps, and he closed the door so quietly behind us that I had to look back to see if it had closed after all.

In his car, he reached under his seat and took out a brown paper bag, fished around, and pulled out a couple of bobby pins and a flashlight.

He actually did it. He used two bobby pins to unlock the side door to Underhill and then used the same pins to open each of the doors inside. My heart leaped. But Lloyd was cautious. I walked around while he called. It was the best chance we'd had yet, and I hoped, I hoped so much, that Tongsu Cho would know something about the men who had taken you and Lloyd to that meeting that night, would know where the men had gone. You had to be with them somewhere.

Dean Olin's office smelled musty, and I found socks under his leather chair. I wondered if Serena knew about those. Lloyd dialed quickly and got the international operator to patch him through to the restaurant, and I heard him ask for Tongsu Cho. Then I heard him describe what he looked like. He held the phone away from him and said to me that the hostess was going back to the kitchen to see if anyone by that name worked there. "Maybe he's using an alias," I suggested.

"Why would he do that?"

"Yes, hello?" he said in English. The hostess must have returned to the phone. Then in Korean, "Yes, it's not a good connection. Could I speak to someone else in the kitchen who might know him? It's really important. Yes, family matter, urgent."

He listened some more and then he thanked her and said he'd call tomorrow. "Different staff tonight for a special event. She said to try tomorrow."

70

I had a dream where a doctor was holding up a graph of your heartbeats. She held it up for me to see, on a large eleven-by-fourteen-inch piece of paper, and she pointed to the parts that showed you were alive and then the straight line where you weren't. "Right here," she said. "This is the moment he died." I cried for you. I cried and cried and cried and couldn't stop crying for you even after I sat up in bed and realized I was in my dorm room. And Lloyd held me and said, "We have to find him, that's all, then these nightmares will stop. I have them too."

71

LOVE, LOVE, LOVE, LOVE. WHY DON'T I DESERVE LOVE? WE HAD A PLAN, YOONA. WE WERE GOING TO FIND JAESUNG. WHY DIDN'T YOU NEED ME ANYMORE?

"You're right, Lloyd. I didn't know what I was doing. But I do now. I do."

There's anguish on his face.

I continue. "It's not too late, and Sax is listening to you. You've got what you wanted. You have proof, and you can free Jaesung."

HE'S LYING TO ME.

"He's trying to help. Come on, if they weren't, they'd be in here by now. You let Daiyu go, and you've shown you're reasonable. That's what matters. And you're a good friend to Jaesung."

HIS ONLY FRIEND.

"His only friend. I'll tell him everything you did to free him. He'll know. Every detail."

I'VE GOT TO GET HIM FREED. THEY'RE NEVER GOING TO LET ME TALK TO THE PRESIDENT. I'VE GOT TO DO IT MYSELF. FLY OVER THERE MYSELF. Lloyd picks up the phone and barks into it. I WANT THAT CAR NOW. AND I WANT A HUNDRED THOUSAND DOLLARS. IT'S A HUNDRED THOUSAND DOLLARS NOW.

"I'll need a few more minutes. The plane is taking a while, Lloyd."

Lloyd pulls the phone to the window, looks out. WHO'S THE MAN WITH THE RED HAT? HE WASN'T THERE BEFORE. AND WHAT'S THAT ARMY TRUCK DOING? IF YOU'RE THINKING ABOUT—BACK OFF WITH THAT TEAR GAS. THERE'S A PREGNANT GIRL IN HERE, REMEMBER.

"Stay calm, Lloyd," I call over to him.

LOOK, I KNOW WHAT I SEE. DON'T TELL ME WHAT I SEE. I KNOW WHAT MY EYES ARE LOOKING AT.

"Let me see, Lloyd. Do I have your permission to see?" I offer and approach the window when he waves me over.

The light is blinding. I shield my eyes and see dozens of police cars, more than I imagined. Their lights are spinning round and round. There are people in uniforms and some with their hands up, holding back people with microphones and vans with antennae on their roofs. In a space up front is a man looking at our window.

"You've seen too many cop shows, Lloyd. I want to work with you. These things take time."

AREN'T YOU TIRED OF SAYING THAT? I'M SICK OF HEARING IT.

"Look, once you let the other three girls walk out like you did with Daiyu, I'll have the car with the money left outside. We can continue to look for your friend. I promise you I'll keep working on that. He matters to you, doesn't he, Lloyd?"

NO. I'M NOT LETTING ANYONE GO. I'VE DONE ENOUGH.

"It's not me, Lloyd," Sax says. "My superior officers thought we were out of time. Believe me, I'm on your side. The pregnancy news will buy you more time. I'm glad for the pregnant girl, believe it or not. I am. It changes everything we usually do. You're right. No tear gas, not even considered here. What about money? I can get you more. A hundred thousand won't last you long. Especially when the girl is pregnant. Is she all right, the pregnant girl? What's her name? Hold on—getting word on something now. Let me get the car, and I'll call you back. Just wait. Don't do anything, we're working this out, Lloyd. Okay?"

GET ME THE CAR. He puts down the handset and pumps the shotgun. The sound is distinct. Detective Sax's voice jumps. "Lloyd, don't be hasty now. You've come this far."

72

We tried again the next night. On the third night we broke into Dean Olin's office, a man who said his name was Tongsu Cho came on the line. "You remember us, the kids from America. You met us on the student tour and then again in Seoul. You took us to a meeting, but you didn't get in the car with us. You sent us to meet these men, for the rally, you remember?" Lloyd pressed Tongsu, repeated himself, agreed that the connection was bad.

I leaned in, and Lloyd put his arm around me and held the receiver between us. "You remember, don't you?" Now we'd find out who had taken you.

The man said he had met some students when he worked on the tour, but that was all. "I just arrived in Seoul this week for work," he said. "How did you know? Do you have news about my father?"

"What happened to your father?"

"I thought you might know. I heard he was sick. I don't know any American students in Seoul."

"We met you, remember in the kitchen on the tour? And you told us about the men losing their fingers in the factory. You lost a finger in the factory. My friend was missing part of his finger, but not from the factory."

"I'm not sure I know what you mean."

"How can you not know? You talked to us, and you talked to my friend. There was a demonstration."

"I'm sorry, but I have to return. It's work hours. Good luck finding your friend. Don't call me again here. I can lose my job."

"But wait, you—we need your help, wait. Wait, hello, Tongsu Cho? I met you—we met you in Korea."

"I don't know who you are," Tongsu said.

"How can he not remember us?" I said.

"Shhh . . . ," Lloyd said to me.

A sickening feeling settled in my stomach. Suddenly, there were footsteps, loud ones, a light came on in the hall. I turned off the flashlight and pulled Lloyd down. We crouched behind the desk, the receiver in his hand. We stayed down until they faded and waited another half hour before we let ourselves out.

The next day Lloyd wouldn't look me in the eye.

"Lloyd, what's going on?" I caught up to him.

"Let's walk. I might be followed."

"You're scaring me."

"They can put listening devices anywhere," he said, surveying the tree branches above us. It was a maple with yellowing leaves, but still full.

"I'm remembering more and more. My head hurts like it's going to burst open, and I can't take it anymore," he said, holding the sides of his head. He ran off.

I followed him and called to him. He kept looking over his shoulder and pivoting around other students. Finally, he slowed enough for me to catch up to him. And then he proceeded to tell me about a Korean man who had been hanging around his block in Queens. The man followed Lloyd to his parents' grocery market and asked people in neighboring shops about him. "They told me he asked. How stupid is he to ask them? He wanted to know if I had friends. Isn't that a weird question? Mr. Lubuni told him to leave me alone. And then he told me what the man said. And he told my parents too."

"You could go to the police with that if you have Mr. Lubuni to verify it."

"The CIA? Is the CIA following me, Yoona?"

"But you said the man was Korean. The KCIA?"

"I think I lost them when I came up here. I think it's safe here. I don't feel watched up here. Not as much. I really don't."

"How could you tell he was following you in the city?"

"It was the same man. I saw the same man. I can feel his eyes on me."

"Why didn't you tell me this before?"

"I was trying to protect you. I hoped we'd find Jaesung before this. Where could he be? What are they doing to him, Yoona?" He was looking everywhere but at me.

"I don't know, but we'll find out. We can go to the police and tell them about the man who's following you. What's he look like?"

"You sound as if you don't believe me."

"I do. I don't know what you mean. You're not making any sense."

"That's what they want us to believe. But you and I know Tongsu Cho exists. Maybe it was another man named Tongsu Cho. Maybe there's another restaurant called Little Pan, or it's a wrong number."

"So many people in Korea have the same name. We have to keep looking."

"Just don't question me about everything as if you don't believe me." He looked at me then, his mouth set in a hard line, and I didn't know if he recognized who I was.

"The man who was following me in the city, he's here. He walked right past you, looked like he was listening to what you were saying, and he's circled around again. He's wearing a red hat." Lloyd was mumbling again. It was the next day, and he refused to let me leave his side, even to go to the bathroom. We were on our way to the lunch truck and the post office. I hoped my mother had been able to send me more money.

"Where?" There were people ahead, alongside, and behind us, all walking away from the dining hall. "I don't see anyone in a red hat. Korean man?"

"Don't be so obvious. Sweatshirt and jeans, red sweatshirt and jeans."

I looked around. He yanked me back around. "Just walk." I hadn't seen anyone in a red sweatshirt. I saw a girl in a red T-shirt and a boy in a black shirt and red shorts, but no one wearing what Lloyd had said.

He was talking again. "He'll expect us to go to this meeting. Especially if you told that girl where we were going. Did you tell her about Korea Society?" Without waiting for my reply, he added, "You did. I knew it. We can't go now. You've got to stop telling people our plans. What did you say, word for word?"

"I didn't know he was on campus. You should have told me. Why are you talking about Korea Society? We agreed we weren't going to go to that."

"These people aren't obvious, Yoona. I wasn't sure until he walked right by you. I wondered if you knew him, and then he walked past. Really casual. And if I wasn't looking for him, I would have missed him. The way they coordinated that attack so I couldn't get out of the car. The way I was locked in that car. We have to find him."

"Korean man, how tall? You have to tell me something. Does he look like a grad student? Older?"

"But there might be more than one. There were two in every car. I didn't want to be split up. I told Jaesung I didn't have a good feeling about it, but he wanted to follow along. He's too trusting. They walked me between them like they thought I'd try to escape."

"What are we going to do? You think he knows who I am? It's not just you he's following?" My heart was jumping out of my chest. Where was the man Lloyd said was following him? I pulled Lloyd's arm off me finally and tried to be discreet about examining the people around us. We were behind the dining hall now, heading toward my dorm.

"I'm sorry, did I hurt you?" he asked and moved his hand toward my head, but I jerked away before he touched me. "I know it's scary, shit, I was scared, but you can't let it show. You know what I mean? You can't let them know you know," he continued. Then he put his hand on his jeans and rubbed it hard. He cleared his throat. "What's wrong with you? Why're you mad at me?"

"I'm not." I was busy looking around. Were we actually in danger?

"Okay, he's gone," Lloyd said. "Slow down."

"How do you know?" I picked up my pace.

"Hey, he's gone. Slow down, will you?"

I stopped abruptly and caught my breath. "We've got to tell the police. Campus first or go straight to the town police? Which?"

"Police? They won't believe us. I tried that in the city. They locked me up and called my parents."

"They can't do that. Why would they do that? When did they do that?"

"Keep your voice down. Yoona, they looked up my record, but it was dumb. It wasn't for anything, but they locked me up. Trust me, they won't believe us."

"What record?"

"You know, community stuff. Forget it; we're on our own."

"Community-activism stuff?"

"Yeah, like that. Hey, Daiyu's always getting hurt, why is that?" He chuckled. I stared at him. Lloyd seemed completely at ease now. He paused. "I thought I saw her just now, that's why."

I let out a breath. I was exhausted, and he must be too. I'd been certain we'd be found under the desk in Dean Olin's room, and I'd be expelled. "She's uncoordinated," I said, answering his question about Daiyu. In front of us, in the doorway of one of the dorms, was an Asian man who looked older than the undergrads. He had on a white button-down shirt and khaki pants. He was smoking in the doorway. Was he one of them?

"They know who we are. The man in the blue hat, one o'clock." Lloyd's voice lowered. A boy I recognized from my Intro to Asian Lit class was staring at us. He always wore a Yankees baseball cap. "He's a student here," I said to Lloyd.

"That's what you think," he returned.

"Where do you know him from?"

"He might have been in the car with us, with me and Jaesung."

"Wait, you said you were in separate cars."

"For part of the trip. They made us switch outside of Seoul."

"You never told me that. You and Jaesung were in the same car for part of the time?"

"I got it. He followed me the first night I got here. The one with the baseball hat."

"You sure about the guy in my Asian lit class? You sure he's the one who's been following you?" I said.

"The first night I came up here."

"You said no one followed you."

"I lost him. But that was him. I remember that hat."

"A hat? You think because he was wearing a hat?"

He looked confused. Then he nodded. "You're right, we've got to split up. I've brought them right to you, and now you're in danger too." He covered his face with his hands.

"Stop, Lloyd, stop, please. We should go to the police. They'll see we're right. They'll see the man outside my dorm. We'll talk and figure it out. Come on, not here," I said. He followed along as if on a leash, his head hanging.

I heard laughter behind us.

It was Daiyu and Faye, holding napkins full of sweet rice cake in their hands. Lloyd fled, and I watched him go with a nervous knot in my stomach. Even as Lloyd's story started to unravel, I told myself he was nervous, that they'd scared him. He'd been through a lot. He was the last one to see you, and you had to be alive. I still wanted to believe you were alive.

73

The sound of helicopters overhead in the distance fills the room. Lloyd's mouth opens, broadcasting bewilderment. Faye starts screaming, "They're coming, finally, oh my god."

"Shut up, Faye," Heather says, but Lloyd doesn't react. The helicopter engine grows louder still.

"Lloyd, what's happening?" I ask and take a few steps toward him. GET BACK ON THE BED, OR ELSE. He's snapped back. I do as he says. He pockets the handgun and stretches for the shotgun leaning against the wall.

"It'll be over soon," I say to myself, but I must have said it aloud too, because Faye agrees and says, "Thank god, we made it."

74

There's a hard knot inside my chest, and it says, as it has said when I've helped my mother after one of my father's rages, *Don't forget this*. And it makes me look at Lloyd now at the window with the same kind of disgust and resolve. I will never put myself in this position with a crazy man again. And there's not even room for you. I'm angry at you for making me vulnerable to someone like him. "He didn't mean any of this," you would say. I know. You would forgive him even this. That day after the blowup at the mandu place, you'd said to me, "We all need to be loved in our own way."

"He can't take out his anger like that," I'd replied.

"He's never known real love, Yoona. But he'll get there. He just needs to know he's loved no matter what. We all need that."

I didn't agree with you, but I didn't want to tell you either. I couldn't admit to you then that I was more like Lloyd than like you.

And this? All this today? Love? Lloyd isn't capable of love. He can call it what he wants, but it's not love. Yeah, I'm sick of it too. The word: love. You and love and love and love. I hate it now because of Lloyd. I hate the word too. Yes, love. He's ruined all of it by constantly using that word. Love? I'm sick of it.

75

My mother sounded concerned when she called. "Your classes going well?" she asked. I didn't tell her I'd been looking for a job and that all of them were minimum wage, which would not be nearly enough for two plane tickets to North Dakota.

"How's Dad?"

"Fine, work is fine."

"Did he get that promotion he wanted? He's not stressed?"

"No. But don't you worry about it. He'll be happy to know you're doing well in your classes. You sure you're doing all right? I mailed you some money. It's not much, but your father insisted I send it. Your father said whatever you need for school. He's very concerned about you, he told me." I couldn't quite believe my father expressed concern, but my mother sounded earnest.

"I love you, Mama," I blurted out. I hadn't planned on it, but there was this feeling, rising over and over, waves of premonition that I'd never see her again.

"What's wrong? Are you sure?"

I steadied my breath. "I miss you, that's all," I said.

"Wait, Willa just came in, she wants to talk to you. Be careful, Yoona, the flu is going around. Rest up," my mother said.

My sister had stopped talking as much about converting me to her religion. She was taking classes at the community college and was hanging out with a boy we both knew named Albert Park. An old friend of ours, actually. The son of a family friend. I didn't like his mother, because she used to look at my mother so pityingly when we ran into her at the grocery store. *How many times can someone break her arm?* her eyes seem to be saying when my mother had yet another cast. But I didn't mind Albert. He wouldn't lure Willa to some fanatical religious sect. She had said she'd never date a Korean guy, so I didn't suspect it was anything more than a friendship. Thinking of Lloyd, I told her I was glad she had a friend. Friends are important, I told her.

Lloyd was up early the next morning, standing watch at the window looking over the parking lot. "There're two of them: the man in the blue hat and another in a red sweatshirt."

I joined him at the window. I didn't see anything but the usual cars in the lot. "Where?"

He pointed to a black sedan. "They've been out there all night."

"But how could they watch us from there? We'd go in and out through the other side—"

"Because they're watching that door too. They're closing in."

I couldn't make out any figures in the car he specified. "I'm going to fail, but I have to show up for my art history test today."

"You can't leave," he begged. I didn't see anyone other than students walking hurriedly to their classes.

"No one's out there," I said.

"They're spies, Yoona. You can't tell when you're being followed by professional spies."

"I've got to take this test," I said. "Daiyu and Faye will walk with me. Heather too."

"Don't stay too long," he said. "Come right back. Eleven o'clock."

"He can't do anything to me with people around. And that boy in my Asian lit class, I'll ask him directly what he was doing last night," I told him.

"We know what he was doing. He was out looking for me."

"Maybe he won't even be in class," I said. "I have to see."

For the next three days, Lloyd refused to leave my room except for short trips to the bathroom. He didn't shower, and he didn't eat unless I brought him food from the food truck. The boy in my Asian lit class had vanished. I reasoned he could be sick with this flu Heather said was going through her chem lecture. "Half of the class has been out sick for the whole week." I still went to the library to check on the news in Korea and had coffee with Serena each day. I made sure to ask what she'd heard about the political unrest in Korea from her father.

"You see her every day," Lloyd said.

"She's my friend, and maybe she can help us. Her parents travel back and forth to Korea a lot. I'm hoping she can help us."

"Maybe they work for the government. Maybe she was sent to this school to spy on you. She's not your friend."

"Lloyd, stop it. What are you saying, really? She says the same thing about you," I said in a moment of hopelessness.

"I'm saying this is bigger than we think." He crawled under the covers and refused to talk to me anymore.

On Friday, October 4, I convinced Lloyd to go to the clinic to see a doctor about his headaches. We walked together, and as we waited for a nurse practitioner, I saw signs warning against pregnancy, STDs, and AIDS, and saw boxes full of condoms for the taking. I was reminded that my own period was late. As of Thursday, it was two weeks late. Still, maybe I'd skip this month. It had happened before when I was stressed, and this month I couldn't shake the flu. When Lloyd refused to go in for his appointment, saying he noticed someone looking at him oddly, I let him go back to the dorm, and I took his place. He agreed I should. "You look worse than me," he announced. It was probably the flu. The waiting room was full of students who were hunched over with congestion and misery.

The nurse reminded me of Willa. I could imagine Willa as a nurse someday, which she wouldn't want to hear from me. She thought nurses were the lackeys of doctors. In her brisk, no-nonsense way, though, the nurse was knowledgeable and thorough. I felt comfortable enough to cry in front of her when she told me the news.

I trudged back to my room and went right under my covers. "That bad, huh?" Lloyd said from his huddled post on the floor under the window.

I don't know why I called your house again. Maybe I was just grasping at straws because the news the nurse had given me felt like nothing was in my hands anymore. Lloyd was making less and less sense and scaring me. I had to know what your uncle and your parents knew to make them believe you were dead. I didn't have any new evidence that you were alive. I just needed to hear it again from someone who loved you. So I could let you go. Your father answered the phone.

"You're cruel, Lloyd," I said to him after the call. I'd gathered all his things and stuffed them into his backpack, and I held it out to him. I didn't want him in my room a minute longer. "It was cruel of you to do this to me."

He was waving his hands, signaling for me to stop. "Yoona, wait, I'm not done. Give me a chance to tell you."

"Tell me what? You said you had something different from the official story, so what is it?" I threw his backpack at his feet. "Get out."

"If you give me a chance, I'll tell you," he said.

I walked to the door to my room and held it open for him. "Out."

"Jaesung wanted to go to this meeting," he began again. "Tongsu Cho, from the kitchen at the camp, remember? Tongsu and his brother. Do you know he had a brother? His brother looked just like him. Like they were identical twins. We talked to him about another meeting—Jaesung met him a bunch of times. I didn't go to all of them, but that night, on the twenty-first, we left together in the same car. Other cars followed us out of Seoul. Four, five, as many as ten, maybe. I saw the lights of the city behind us, and we drove for a long time."

"You said you were in different cars. Jaesung's father said it was the same car. He said you were driving, and you feel guilty because you were behind the wheel and you had been drinking."

"There was an accident. The car behind us, which didn't have me or Jaesung in it—are you listening? That car was hit broadside, not mine and not Jaesung's. His car was in the lead with two guys we met before, mine was in the middle, and the one behind us got struck at an intersection. It was remote, and it was weird because there weren't other cars on the road, and out of nowhere a dump truck clips the car I'm in and slams the car behind us, and that car gets knocked off the road and turned on its side. We all stop. All three cars. I tried to get out, but I couldn't budge the door. The men on the other side of me, two guys, get out of their side and shut the door, and when I go after them, the door is locked. And that's when I knew something was really wrong. I'm locked in. My door isn't jammed. I bang on the divider up to the front, but there's silence. I figure he must have left the car too, and then I think, as the car on its side starts to smoke, that I'm going to die in this car."

"If there's a divider and you're in the backseat, how do you know the first car stopped? And where was Jaesung?"

"You're right. I don't know. But then I heard sirens right away, firemen opened the car door and helped me out, and they told me my friend is dead. But when I look around, there's no car up front, just mine and the one behind me on its side. And the body they take away on a stretcher that's burned, with a cover thrown over it, that body isn't

Jaesung's. I saw the arm hanging off, and it was a suit jacket arm, black. The smell was horrible."

I felt empty. "Of course it was his. It could have been burned black."

"I know it's hard to believe. We were taken in the same car for a while, but then they separated us. It was their plan. They only needed one of us. That's what must have happened."

"You should go. I want you to leave."

"It wasn't him, Yoona," Lloyd said. "The car was smoking, but there wasn't a fire. Jaesung was wearing short sleeves like me, you remember that day? It was so hot. I saw it clearly. An ambulance came, and the paramedics forced me to go to the hospital even though I said I was fine, but it was weird. I'm telling you: it wasn't Jaesung. When his parents came to the hospital to talk to me later—that's the other thing, they wouldn't let me leave right away—"

"You were injured. That's not hard to understand."

"But that's the thing: I wasn't. Nothing was wrong with me, but they gave me drugs to make me sleep, and I swear it was like they wanted to confuse me."

"How would you know? You said the truck clipped you."

"I'm telling you I was fine. Nothing was wrong with me, but they kept me for days in that hospital."

"For your parents to come and to make sure you were all right."

They'd kept him for two days in the hospital. I believed they were right; something was wrong with Lloyd. My hopes for you were fading. Tears pricked my eyes.

"You don't believe me," he said.

"You had a head injury. Jaesung's dad said you had swelling in your brain." It was hard to speak. I felt like I was being strangled.

He threw up his hands and shook his head. "That does not mean I didn't see everything. I know what happened. How can you not believe me? I thought you, of all people, you would know I'm telling the truth."

"You think you know, but you were unconscious for two days."

"Why would I lie about this? Don't forget there were fire trucks but no fire."

"There was a fire. You're confused. You had a head injury."

"He's alive, Yoona. Jaesung didn't die in that car."

"I can't listen to you anymore."

"It's a conspiracy—they've convinced Jaesung's dad. I don't know how, but I'm going to find out."

"Just leave me alone, Lloyd. Please. Go home."

I could feel him staring at me for a long minute, but I refused to meet his eyes. Finally, he left, and I curled up on the bed and tried to sleep.

The nurse said it was normal that I felt nauseated, that it was just the stage I was in, but I didn't wholly believe her. To my mind, everything in me was rejecting this pregnancy. I was woken hours later by Lloyd's voice calling from the other side of the door, begging me to let him in. "My legs, Yoona, my legs are cramping on this cold floor. Yoona, let me in, let me in."

"Go home, Lloyd. Just go home."

"Don't do this, don't shut me out."

I pulled the blanket over my head to drown out his words.

The next thing I knew, the phone was ringing. I recognized Willa's voice. "How bad is it?" I said.

"Oh—" she said, and I heard her let out a breath. When she spoke again, she spoke more slowly. "It's not what you think. She has pneumonia, Yoona. It was a cold that just turned into pneumonia somehow. Her fever was 104, so we took her to the emergency room."

"I'll be there as soon as I can," I said.

"Don't come now. Just stay by a phone, and I'll let you know if it gets any worse. The doctor is supposed to talk to us soon."

"Are you sure that's all it was? No fights?" I said.

"I've been in every night. Albert's been busy. I promise you it's not Dad's fault this time."

Hearing her acknowledge it, even though it was reassuring news, made my throat close with grief. "I'm coming anyway," I said.

"Yoona, by the time you get here, they might have let her go home."

"Okay." I sat back down, deflated. Maybe she was right. She hung up, and I held the receiver dumbly in my hands.

There was a clatter of knocks on the door. I opened the door to find Lloyd leaning against the frame on the other side. "I heard the phone. Everything all right?"

"No," I replied and closed it. He knocked harder. I opened the door again. Lloyd was sitting on the floor, bracing his hand against the doorframe.

"Then it's your mom, isn't it? I'll drive you. It's four hours, right? We'll be at your house by ten thirty."

"Willa says to wait."

"I'm still your friend. Let me help you."

"Just go home, Lloyd. Go back to your parents. Go back to Queens."

"You don't mean it."

"Go home. Please."

"You're upset. Please, don't shut me out. You promised Jaesung you wouldn't do that anymore."

"How do you know that?"

"He told me. Who do you think talked to him after you wrecked his heart each time?" He looked up at me as if I were the most unreasonable person in the world. "I'll be waiting in my car downstairs for you, and I'll drive you to the hospital. It's the least I can do for you. We're in this together."

He said more, and I bit my lip so I wouldn't lash out at him again. It was all I could do to stand there with my hand gripping the doorknob. Heather must have had an early class, because her door opened, and she walked out and saw us. Lloyd saw her too, and her smile turned into concern. "No need to call the RA," I said to her, loud enough for a person walking down the hall to turn his head in our direction.

"I'll be waiting downstairs," Lloyd said, standing up, his backpack in his hands. I closed the door when he had cleared the threshold. The bus station ticket office opened at seven, so I waited and then called for the next bus going in the direction of Lakeburg.

76

The phone rings. ANSWER IT, Lloyd barks, still looking out the window. The helicopter engines have grown more distant. A constant drone now.

I pick it up and hear Sax's voice. "Sorry about that, someone tipped off the Scranton news crews. I've got Dick Thornburgh's office willing to talk."

"Hurry," I say.

"Who's this? Where's Lloyd?"

Lloyd grabs the phone from me and shoves me toward the bed. I GAVE YOU THE GIRL, AND YOU CALL IN MORE POLICE? IS THAT HOW YOU WANT TO PLAY THIS GAME? I'VE GOT THREE MORE IN HERE, REMEMBER? IF YOU THINK YOU CAN— He drops the phone and grabs Heather, his arm around her neck, and shrieks, TELL HIM I'M NOT AFRAID TO ADD HEATHER TO THE LIST.

Heather sputters, pulling at his arm, which he jerks tight and releases, jerks again.

I pick up the phone and offer it to him. "You tell him. You're the one he's negotiating with. You're the one who holds all the cards. Tell him to make the helicopters back off. Lloyd, for Jaesung. Diplomacy. Keep calm." I nod and continue to hold out the phone.

He releases Heather and shoves her to the floor before grabbing the phone from me. I SWEAR I'M—

That's when Heather, even with her hands still taped together, springs up and scrambles for the door. Faye backs away, and Lloyd launches toward

Heather. I reach for him and find his leg, and then he kicks me, and I land on the floor and try to get to my feet, but my legs don't cooperate. Did she make it? "What's happening, what's going on, Lloyd?" Sax's tinny voice is the only one I hear, coming from the receiver on the floor beside me.

77

The Greyhound bus stopped at half a dozen places along the way. I took a taxi from the bus station to the hospital and walked into the lobby at two thirty in the afternoon. The receptionist looked up with a smile and asked me who I was visiting, and I couldn't remember my mother's name. The white-haired woman at the desk looked at me tenderly. "Are you all right, dear?" she said.

And a voice at my side said, "Soojin Lee," and I saw that it was Lloyd. I didn't have the strength to be angry at him. The bus ride had been long, and I'd waited another hour at the station for a taxi to take me to the hospital. I scowled at him and headed for the third floor, as the receptionist directed. He followed.

Willa and my father were sitting by the window in the waiting area, looking out. And I was struck by how devastated my father looked. I'd never seen him at a loss. Even after his episodes in the house, he'd take his seat in his La-Z-Boy chair in front of the television and act like nothing had happened. No apology. As if he were perfectly justified in what he'd done to my mother. But now in the hospital, he looked like a child, and his small stature added to that impression. He loomed large in my mind, but only because of his bellowing voice and his quick hands, which seemed to push and punch and be everywhere at once, attacking my mother. Now, as I neared, he and Willa stood up, and he held out his arm awkwardly, but I didn't go any closer to him. Willa gave me a weak smile, so I knew she was relieved I had come. I saw her look beyond me to where Lloyd was standing near the entrance to the waiting area. I turned back to my sister and father. "Can I see her?"

"They made us leave because they had put her on a ventilator." His voice was small.

"They'll come back out and let us know when we can go back in," Willa explained. "How'd you get here?"

I sat down at her words. I hoped I wasn't too late. I looked over at Lloyd, who had taken a seat now as far from us as possible despite the empty chairs in between. "A friend from school," I explained.

That seemed to be an acceptable answer. My father said he would go to thank him, but I told him it wasn't necessary. He winced at my words, but I didn't care. He had no right to pretend to be the gracious father now. Exasperated, I walked over to Lloyd. "Come meet my father."

"You hate him," he said.

Willa was talking earnestly with my dad, so I didn't think they heard, but I saw others closer to us in the waiting room freeze. "What's the matter with you?" I barked and stomped away from him to sit near my father and sister.

We waited for another half hour before the nurse said we could go in. "Two at a time," she warned and looked at Lloyd, who had moved to a chair closer to us by now.

I was irritated by him. "He's not family," I told her.

My father said Willa and I should go in first. We didn't disagree. "She'd want to see you two," he said.

78

Here is where I tell you I told Lloyd things about my family that I didn't tell you in Korea. He knows about my father's rages. One night after he returned to Weston, after Tongsu Cho said he didn't remember you or Lloyd or me, when we despaired, my mother called on the phone. After I hung up, Lloyd asked me what was wrong, and I said I felt as if I was failing her and you. And Lloyd's reaction that night and now in the hospital was the one I didn't want you to have. Where you looked at my family with prejudice and disdain. And me too—where you looked at me that way too, as a coward who had failed to protect my mother. I wanted you to see me always the way you had in Korea, as someone who stood up for those who couldn't stand up for themselves.

79

My mother used to tell me and Willa when we were little girls how my father suffered. "Forgive him," she said. "He loves you, and he wants the best for you, but it's too much. This world is too much for us." Those were the nights the television flashed lights on the walls of the living room, and we had to be quiet, but we had to be in the room too, to keep our father company after his long day at work. Our mother peeled oranges, taking off the thin skin of each section for pure pulp.

80

Nothing prepared me for seeing my mother in the intensive care room full of curtains and machines. She was on a ventilator, and seeing her with her eyes closed and her facial muscles slack, I realized I'd never seen her asleep in my entire life. How could that be?

"She looks like that because she's not asleep," the nurse explained as if reading my mind, adjusting buttons and dials on the machines around us.

"Can she hear us?" Willa said.

"They sedate patients before putting in the ventilator." she answered and then left us. I held my mother's hand, trying not to stare at the two intravenous lines taped down to the top. The skin around the tape gleamed as if my mother had applied her daily moisturizing cream minutes earlier. Her tender, smooth skin was her particular beauty. An irony that my father had damaged it routinely. I turned away. The doctor came in and said we would have to wait and see now. They'd done all they could.

When we returned to the waiting room to send our father in, Albert was talking with him. Albert recognized me and gave me a hug when I walked over. "I'm sorry," he said. I'd had a fantasy when I was a child that Albert would marry Willa, and they'd make me their child and move me away from our father's fits. She and Albert were four years older than I was. Albert was the perfect peacemaker. He'd stood up for me in school once when some kids my age made fun of what I had brought for lunch. With his Clark Kent glasses, Albert had been my idea of a superhero. Willa didn't consider him dating material, though they were in the same grade and it was obvious he had eyes only for her. I was glad for his sake that she was spending more time with him. Albert was a good friend.

I saw my sister squeeze his hand and drop it in a hurry. Willa took charge. She figured out a schedule where she and Dad would go home for a few hours and return at dinnertime for us. And then I'd go get some rest and sleep at the house and come back for her and our dad in the morning. "You'll need your sleep if you have to drive back," she said, and she nodded toward Lloyd, who was still sitting by the door. I regretted my earlier harsh dismissal of him. "What are you going to do with him?" she said.

"He convinced me to come and drove me here. He's trying to be respectful," I explained, because I knew Willa was judging him the way I had.

"Good friend," Albert summed up. His opinion meant a lot to me, and I was glad when he walked over with me. Lloyd stood up and extended his hand to Albert.

"I've heard about you," Lloyd said, which made me blush. Albert's amused eyes flicked in my direction for a second.

"Thanks for helping out," Albert returned. Lloyd relaxed. "So I hear you kids have the first shift? Want me to bring you anything from the real world? Real coffee?" He lifted his eyebrows. I told him that would be perfect.

Later, when Willa, my dad, and Albert returned to the hospital, Lloyd and I went to the house. Every hour or so I'd gone in to check on my mother, who remained unconscious. It rattled me to see her that way.

We had enough money to go out for watery soup, crackers, and coffee at a corner café. Lloyd and I split a piece of chocolate cake that was so dry it crumbled into tiny pieces—but it bought us a place to sit and try not to panic about my mother's condition for a few hours.

I couldn't shake the feeling that I was in fact in an alternate universe. Somewhere out there, I was someplace else, and my mother wasn't in the hospital for pneumonia. The waiter, Mike, yelled that it was good to see me again, and I thought how different I was from a few months ago before I'd gone to Korea, before I'd met you and Lloyd. Now my mother was on the line, and dread hit me like a sledgehammer as it had at the clinic.

"He knows you?" Lloyd said. "Jaesung would be surprised."

"Why?" I said.

"You're not listening," Lloyd said and peered at me as if I'd fainted, and I wondered if I'd lost consciousness of this moment. Time was folding in on itself.

"What are you talking about, Lloyd?" I tried to make my voice brisk and authoritative.

He got up, slid over to my side of the booth, and gave me a hug, but I pulled away. "It's going to be okay," he said, but he seemed to be talking to himself more than me. "Listen, I think we lost them when we drove here. Maybe that's the thing to do, keep moving. I hadn't thought of that. Only way to be safe." I let him mumble, but I wasn't listening.

At the house there was an awkward moment concerning where we'd sleep. Even though my father and Willa weren't home, I couldn't sleep with Lloyd near me, not even in my room. I didn't think he'd assume he would, but he followed me to my room and folded back the covers. "I'm exhausted," he announced. "We need to talk." He lay down on my bed and put his hands behind his head like a pillow.

Fury curled my hands. I twisted the doorknob. "Get out, Lloyd. Can't you see I need a break?"

"A break? Do you think those men are taking a break from tracking us? Is this some game to you?"

"It's my house, Lloyd. My sister and father could walk in at any time."

"I know you're mad at me, but let's get past it. For now, while you're in this crisis with your mother, I think we should calm down. I won't abandon you, no matter how hard you push me away. Friends don't do that to other friends. I know you're quick to cut ties. Jaesung said you had a problem with that, so I'll pretend you didn't say those fucked-up things to me back at Weston. I'll give you another chance."

"Stop talking about him."

"Why? Because you'd rather he were dead?"

"How dare you say that?"

"Something's different about you," he said. "It's like you're a robot. I don't think Jaesung would understand."

"You don't know what he would understand. Get out," I said.

Fatigue threatened to knock me over. He was shouting again. "You never believed me. That's the only way you can talk to me like this. The only way, because you don't think it's real. You don't care about him. You're cutting him off like you did all those times in Korea. You're breaking your promise to him."

"Get out, Lloyd," I said. It seemed to be the only statement I could make in any form. I repeated it over and over again. I held open the door and stood there.

The air in the room swirled as he bounded up from the bed, stomped to the doorway, stormed through it, and slammed it shut behind him. That was fine. I was used to doors slamming in my house. Without changing my clothes, I crawled into bed and closed my eyes. I felt my shoulders heave and realized I was crying myself to sleep. I gave in to sheer fatigue. The smell of the laundry detergent my mother used, the one I remembered throughout my childhood, lavender and something they called "spring wind" on the label, filled my senses and carried me to sleep.

I woke to the smell of bacon and eggs. Lloyd held a tray in front of him. My first thought was that my mother was in the kitchen. "Should she be cooking?" I said.

"Should who be cooking?" he replied.

"Why are you here?"

He shrugged. "Willa called from the hospital. Your mom is awake," he said.

It all came back to me. The hospital. I hurried to the bathroom to wash my face and then returned to look for clean clothes to wear.

"You've got to eat something," Lloyd said from the bedroom door.

"I should go," I mumbled and dug into my dresser for folded shirts. I had no time to deal with Lloyd. Something in here must be dark and plain, but my high school self seemed to have had a fascination with bright colors in frilly ruffled material. Such silly mall-store clothes in peppy candy colors. I was forced to wear a tank top with daisies and jeans.

"I remember you wore this the day I met you. I like it better than the stuff you wear now," he said. "College girls think it's intellectual to wear plain things. You look better in patterns, Yoona."

I ignored him and went back to poking around for a sweater. I felt his hand on my shoulder and whirled around. "Stop touching me," I said.

"You have a thread—wait," he said and plucked something from my shirt, but I didn't see anything between his thumb and forefinger, and I wondered if he was lying. He followed me to my parents' room, where I found a sweater in my mother's closet. It was a rough shawl-necked cardigan with strands of gray- and mustard-colored thread woven through thick maroon wool, one of the few things my mother had brought from Korea when she'd immigrated. I'd thought it ugly, but she wore it late at night over her nightgown. I decided to wear it now over my shirt.

"What's with all the guns?" Lloyd said. I kept forgetting he was in my house.

I turned to him now and let out a sigh. "What are you talking about?" I said, and I knew I sounded annoyed.

"These," he said, pointing to parts of a handgun on my father's dresser.

"He collects them. Goes to garage sales and things like that. He's obsessed with guns," I said.

"It's in pieces," he said.

"He's got ones that work someplace," I said just to shut him up.

"He's an asshole who glorifies guns," Lloyd said. "I hate that he hurt your mom, that he did that to you."

"You can go now. I'm fine." I was standing at the front door, ready to lock up the house, and he was standing in the middle of the room, judging my family.

153

"You said you hated him. I don't blame you. He's a coward. The worst kind. Look at him and his guns. Probably doesn't even know what a real gun is."

"He knows," I said and then regretted it even as I wondered why I was defending my father.

"You mean the shotgun and the handgun he has here?" Lloyd opened the front hall closet, reached up to the top shelf, and then thrust the handgun, laid flat in his palm, at me. "He hides them in obvious places."

"Get that shit away from me," I said and went outside.

A minute later he was outside too, and I locked the door after him, and we walked to his car. He knew the way back to the hospital without my directions. "Go home," I said to him when he pulled up at the entrance. I tried a lighter touch. "I appreciate this, but I'm okay. Please, go home to the city, Lloyd."

"I don't believe you. You're overreacting because of your father. I'm not your father," he said.

"You're crazy," I said without meaning to. It just struck me as I stared at him that he hadn't heard anything I'd said these past three days. I wondered whether he had ever heard me.

"Stop pushing me away. I'll handle your dad, don't worry. I know how to deal with bullies."

Anything I said would be a waste of time. I felt his eyes on me as I slammed his car door and walked through the front entrance of Lakeburg General. I repeated to myself over and over again to remain calm and assured myself Lloyd would leave. He had to leave. I'd invited him into my life, and now I wanted him gone.

I was mad at all men. As I made my way through that hospital to my mother's room, I was mad at everyone, even you. That comment Lloyd made about the clothes I'd worn in Korea made me wonder about what you'd think of me now. But of course that wasn't the only thing.

I had to stop in the bathroom to throw up. I knew I had to deal with being pregnant. I had to figure out what to do before it was too late.

81

The way to the door is clear. I can see that, even from my view from the floor. Lloyd didn't push the desk back in front of the door after Daiyu left, and Heather takes advantage of that now and turns the knob before Lloyd yanks her away by her hair. She's thrown back into Faye, who rolls away to avoid the collision. Lloyd isn't satisfied with that. He jumps on top of Heather and starts hitting her with a hard object in his hand.

Finally I'm on my feet, and I'm pulling at Lloyd's coat. "Stop, Lloyd. Stop, you're killing her."

I don't think about it even as Lloyd takes a second to hit me, the metal of the gun slams into my head, and I'm knocked to the floor for the second time. But I feel a strange exhilaration even though I can't get myself to move from where I've landed. It's what I should have done when my father hit my mother, what I've always willed myself to do, and here I'd done it. I hear Faye screaming and Lloyd making this *ooph* sound as if he can't catch his breath, and I wonder, *What is that pile of clothes he's thrashing on my bed?*

And then I know it's not clothes. I push myself up with my hands, and I scan the room for the shotgun. It's on the floor next to Lloyd's feet. I crawl to it.

Lloyd tilts the handgun so it's aimed at Heather's temple and stares at me. WHAT DO YOU THINK YOU'RE DOING? he says as if there isn't a bleeding, moaning girl beneath him. PUT THAT GUN DOWN.

82

When I walked into the ICU's curtained-off section they had for my mother, the drugs they'd given her must have been taking their toll. She sounded agitated and upset. The tubes and catheter had been taken out. She said to my father, "Why is Yoona here?" as if I couldn't answer for myself.

"She came to see you," he answered.

"Well, go back to school. I don't want her grades to suffer because of me. And what about Willa?"

"You're so silly, Ma," Willa said, bending close. "I'm going to the community college, remember? I'm still going."

"You promised me." She looked at me and repeated herself.

"I know, Ma," I said. "I know."

"Make them go," she said, looking only at my father.

"You're very sick, Ma," I said.

"I'm not. I'm fine. See?" She tried to raise herself from the bed and then gave up, letting herself sink into the mattress.

"They'll be back for Thanksgiving," he answered, nodding to us.

My mother closed her eyes. "Yes," she said.

"Do you remember what happened, Ma?" I asked.

She nodded.

The doctor came in then and said that the worst was past.

"I'll call. Go back to school, like she said," Willa said.

"I can stay so you can take a break," I said.

"Dad and I are going back to the house to sleep. Albert's promised to come by. So go back to Weston. You heard the doctor."

I sat with my mother for a few more minutes, and when she was able to squeeze my hand, I knew she was better. Relief flooded through me. She was going to be fine. "Go back to school," she said, and her eyes filled with tears, and she nodded until I nodded with her and promised her I would.

Outside Lloyd was still in the car with his eyes trained on the doors. I walked to his side of the car, where his window was lowered. He raised his eyebrows. "So? How is she?"

I told him she was going to be okay, and he seemed visibly relieved. It softened me toward him. I tried to make amends. "I'm sorry I snapped at you," I said.

"Apology accepted. Get in, let's go back to school now," he said.

"You need to go home, Lloyd."

He looked away and then leaned over and released the passenger-side door. "I can't leave you here like this. The bus was a nightmare. Admit it."

I saw a trace of the Lloyd who'd found me at the bottom of the stairs after the party in the student union at the beginning of the semester. The one who said I could sit there and he'd sit with me, and everything else could wait.

Lloyd drove me back to campus, and I told him before I got out of the car that he should go back to the city.

He stared straight ahead. "You're saying you don't need me anymore."

"That's not what I'm saying. We'll always be friends. And we'll still talk. Maybe I have to go back to Korea, and you could go with me. We can't know what happened to him from here."

"How do you know how you'll feel later today or even tomorrow? You'll need me. I think I should stay for a while, and then after we go to your house again for Thanksgiving, after that I'll feel better about leaving you here by yourself."

"Thanksgiving? You're not going home with me."

"Your mom is in the hospital, Yoona. Everything isn't fine. You need me. You're in danger."

"The boy you think was following you isn't in class anymore. We're not in danger, Lloyd."

157

"That's not proof of anything. It only proves he was never a student to begin with. You're in danger."

"I haven't changed my mind. You can't stay in my room anymore."

He was silent. I opened the car door. "I'm sorry I was mad at you. I'll call you in a few weeks," I told him.

"If it's about the room, I'll find another place to stay." He leaned toward me, and I jerked backward. "It was only going to be a hug," he said.

"I'm tired, Lloyd. I've got to go," I said and got out of the car.

"You'll change your mind."

"Go home," I said and slammed the door shut. His car took off, spinning its tires. I went up to my room, collapsed on the bed, and slept like the dead. Isn't that the expression? I slept without dreaming.

83

The side of my face throbs, and touching it makes it worse. It's not over. None of it is. Outside there's still the staccato thud of helicopters. Heather's attempt at escape has left her gasping for breath, her face a bloody mess. Lloyd pushes the muzzle into Heather's head, and she cries out. My friends are going to die if I don't do something. No one can save us. Sax is doing nothing but giving Lloyd time to kill each of my friends. Lloyd is not getting a car or a conversation with the president. The hard knot in my chest unravels. You would say there's got to be a way. I hold the shotgun out to him.

"You dropped this, thought you might want it," I say. Nothing about it sounds truthful, but I have to think of something. Faye has her arms crossed over her knees, and she doesn't look up. Lloyd lets Heather collapse on the bed, then he wipes the gun in his hand against his coat, and there's a red smear now against the gray wool. I try not to look at the blood too closely. He gets to his feet as if the effort exhausts him, and takes the shotgun from me. Something about this is familiar—the feel of the gun, something about the gun.

I approach the bed and stifle a sob as I examine Heather. *Stay still, Heather,* I say silently to her. I know touching her will make her hurt more. "She needs medical help," I tell Lloyd. My mother didn't have head contusions like Heather seems to have, but Lloyd opened up a cut on her head, and she's bleeding.

IT'S A FUCKING BRUISE, SHUT UP.

"No, she needs stitches. Look, she's losing consciousness. She's going to die," I tell him.

STOP LYING. I HARDLY TOUCHED HER.

I turn away from Heather so I can control my voice. "Lloyd, of course you know all about injuries. Let's ask the detective for a car, and let's go somewhere. This can't be good for the baby. Ask him for a car and some money, and we'll drive to Canada, and we'll keep looking for Jaesung. Maybe they'll listen to us in Canada. But I need you to help me with this baby. Are you still willing to do that?"

PICK UP THE PHONE. ASK ABOUT THE CAR. Lloyd stands up from the bed and backs away.

Sax's voice comes through. "Almost, Lloyd. Can I speak to the girls? We heard some disturbing noise. What's happened? Anyone hurt?"

"She's bleeding too much, she needs help," I tell him.

"Who's bleeding? Lloyd?" Sax asks.

SHUT UP. SHE DESERVED IT. SHE'S BEEN ASKING FOR IT. DID YOU SEE WHAT SHE DID? This is directed at me and Faye. I wipe my hands on my jeans.

"Lloyd, they want to send some people in, I can't hold them back," Sax says, and it's a plea. If he's been an expert negotiator for twenty years, why does he need to plead?

I put my hands on my stomach. "All of this is upsetting to the baby," I say. He narrows his eyes at me.

"You're responsible for all this, Yoona," Faye hisses with her head still buried in her arms.

"Let me see," I say and put the phone down and move over to Heather.

"You killed her, you murderer," Faye screams.

"What's going on in there, Lloyd?" Sax shouts.

SHUT THE FUCK UP OR YOU'LL BE NEXT.

"You're a monster, a fucking monster. You had to hit her that hard? You just had to?" Faye continues.

YOU THINK BEING A MURDERER IS THE WORST THING YOU CAN BE? he howls at Faye. KNOWING YOU STAND BY WHEN PEOPLE—THOUSANDS, HUNDREDS OF THOUSANDS—ARE BEING MURDERED. THAT'S WHAT YOU'RE DOING RIGHT NOW.

"Lloyd, I can't protect you if they come in," Sax says, his voice calmer now.

GET ME MY CAR.

Sax's voice sounds again: "You've broken your promise, Lloyd."

Lloyd waves the phone at me. TELL HIM IT'S A SUPERFICIAL WOUND, THAT'S ALL IT IS.

"Wait, Lloyd, if someone is hurt, we have to talk about that," Sax says. "I can't protect you if they go in."

I'M NOT NEGOTIATING ANYMORE.

"Send out the girl you hurt, or there won't be a car."

OH, THERE WON'T? Lloyd's voice is sarcastic. YOU SURE?

"We're close to the end, and this is what you do? I've gotten through to the White House. I've spoken to the president's aide, and he agrees that this is an international concern. The president's arranged for you to have special immunity as a temporary agent for the FBI. We've located a minivan to transport all of you to the airport, and we're packing it with money now for your use. I told you, I haven't lost anyone yet, and I don't intend to today."

NEVER HEARD ABOUT A TEMPORARY FBI AGENT.

"Serena told me they have them," I agree.

"But the president wants to make sure no one dies. That would cancel everything."

Lloyd puts the phone in my hand. TELL HIM. And then he hurries to the window.

"She's breathing," I tell Sax.

"You're pregnant, are you?" Sax asks.

"If you can get someone from the State Department to talk to him, even if it's not the president—"

"Your name? The names of the others with you?" Sax interrupts me.

I tell him before Lloyd can make it back over to take the phone from me. I KNEW PRESIDENT REAGAN WOULD UNDERSTAND. CARTER'S A WIMP, BUT I KNEW PRESIDENT REAGAN WOULD BELIEVE ME. I'M READY TO BE PART OF THE FBI JUST TO GET JAESUNG FREE.

"There are instructions in the car. Drive the car to Wilkes-Barre/Scranton Airport. That's the way we handle all our agents. There are special instructions in the glove compartment." Sax speaks slowly, as if he's passing along a password to Lloyd.

IS THAT WHY THE MAN WITH THE RED HAT IS OUTSIDE WITH YOU? HE'S FBI, ISN'T HE?

"Can't fool you, Lloyd. That's the kind of thinking President Reagan says he needs in the FBI."

HE'S CIA THEN?

"You were right the first time. FBI. Sent to make sure those North Koreans didn't kidnap any more American students."

I can't believe what I'm hearing. Was Lloyd correct all along? But then I see the fear on Faye's face, and I know Sax is playing a dangerous game. A temporary FBI agent? But Lloyd nods along to everything Sax says. If Lloyd suspects he's lying, what will Lloyd do to us?

84

I woke up having slept for twelve hours straight. The nurse had told me I could make an appointment at a clinic in Scranton. It was a two-hour bus ride. I called them, and their earliest available appointment was in fifteen days. I'd be nine weeks pregnant. Though the receptionist told me I was still eligible for the D&C, I felt panic surge in me. I couldn't wait another day with this knowledge. Fifteen days seemed impossible.

"With so many closures, everyone is coming to us. October twenty-second is the best we can do," she explained when I pleaded with her to move up the date. "Come in at nine a.m. and speak to a counselor about your choices. They're very good at helping people here. They'll explain everything then. It'll be fine," she said. I hung up not feeling anything would be fine. My life was on hold. Classes didn't matter, Lloyd vanished from my consciousness, and other college students seemed to have no idea how lucky they were not to have what I had hanging over their heads. My life had veered toward a cliff. If you were dead, this might become the child we could have had together, but I wasn't ready, I'm sorry, but I was not in any way ready, and I couldn't handle this. Not any of it. I needed my life back.

I started walking without an idea of where I was going. Downtown I stopped in a diner and ate a huge breakfast of pancakes and eggs. I was craving ice cream, so even though it was morning, I ordered that too. The waitress raised her eyebrows. "Why not?" she said.

Eventually, by afternoon, I made it back up to campus. A large group had gathered by the founder's statue. Someone was speaking into a bullhorn about the divestment movement. Faye was standing by the walkway, listening. I felt such relief to see her, but I felt guilty too. I couldn't explain. "Where have you been?" she said when I walked up.

I told her about my mom. She listened and told me about her father's illnesses over the years. She'd never shared much about her life at home. I'd spent all this time with Serena and not much with Faye,

Heather, or Daiyu. And yet these three had welcomed me from the beginning. Faye was headed to the shantytown, where Heather and Daiyu were working on their makeshift house. I walked with her.

The roof was the first thing I saw. A roof fashioned out of aluminum sheets and plywood boards nailed together for walls. Large metal staples held smaller fragments together. The door was special, with a circular window that Faye said Heather had cut with a jigsaw. I traced it with my finger in awe. Between studying and all their clubs and activities, how had they managed this? My friends had made a rain-impervious shelter, complete with a decorative front door, with a small bench inside. "Daiyu made the bench," Heather said when I opened the door and greeted her. "And the floor is our next project. We really need a solid floor."

"I think these houses are supposed to make us feel bad for people who live in places like this," I said. "Don't get carried away."

"Good point," she answered, laughing.

Heather said people were nervous about the sit-in, and there was pressure from the first round of exams in classes, and stupid fights were breaking out on campus. Faye joined in, saying someone had emptied someone else's backpack at the library, scattering notes and books between shelves. A girl nearby said she'd seen an Asian guy run out of the stacks with a can of spray paint.

I left them to head to the library a few minutes later. I meant to get a quick sandwich at the lunch truck, but found myself famished and ordered two, plus a large chocolate milkshake. On my way back to my dorm, I took a shortcut through the back lot of a dorm for upperclassmen and heard the sound of something heavy being dropped over and over again. I saw someone who looked like Lloyd pulling garbage bags out of a large green dumpster. I tried to get closer to see if it actually was him, but when he turned in my direction, I stepped behind a van. When I heard the sound of bags being moved resume, I looked around the van and saw Lloyd open them one by one, fish around inside, and take out articles of clothing. He pulled on pants over his pants and then took a long gray wool coat and shrugged it on, folding the wide flaps over his chest.

I backed away and retraced my steps to walk the long way to my room. The image of Lloyd pawing through the dumpster remained even as I tried to block it out. I made myself focus and called the hospital, and they let me talk to Willa, who was in my mother's room. She said our mother was sleeping, and Albert was keeping Willa company. "They think maybe tomorrow they might send her home," Willa said. This was good news at least.

The next morning, I went to the clinic to talk to the nurse again, and I saw Lloyd running past the shantytown. Something clattered out of his hand, but he still ran, and when I came upon it, I saw that it was a can of red spray paint.

Later that day, Daiyu told me that a section of the shantytown, including their house, had been vandalized, along with the statue of Weston's founder in the quad. Someone had scrawled a line of red across the houses that read "Hypocrites." Around Theodore Weston's neck, someone had sprayed red paint in a gory depiction of a beheading.

"Who could have done this?" Daiyu said.

"I don't know, but Serhan says red paint was stolen from the art studio last night," Faye offered.

"I've never heard of Serhan," I said.

"Her new boyfriend," Daiyu said. "He's Turkish and tells her all these Turkish sayings. He's so cute."

"You think everyone is cute," Heather said.

"He's a writer—he's all about fate and romantic sayings," Faye said.

85

My watch says it's been only three hours, but it seems like an entire twenty-four have passed. Lloyd stands looking out the window, but to the side. I'd read somewhere that they put snipers on hills to shoot people like him, people who take hostages like this. Lloyd seems to know this too, because he never puts himself in front of the window. All we can do is wait for what happens next. Maybe once we try to leave the building, Sax will have a plan to help us. The drive to the airport is an hour. I wonder if my parents are on their way to Weston by now.

The phone rings again. Lloyd slides over to the phone and nods before holding out the receiver to me. HE WANTS YOU.

Detective Sax speaks in a tone that makes me feel sorry for him. "A shotgun and a handgun are missing from those registered to your father. Are those the weapons in the room with you?"

Everyone in the room can hear, but Lloyd has returned to the window and doesn't look in my direction. The shotgun is in his hands, and I realize now why it and the handgun looked familiar. "Tell my parents I'm okay," I reply.

"I'm sorry to tell you, your parents were the victims of gunshot wounds last night," Sax says.

"What do you mean?" I'm trying to understand the words "victims" and "wounds." "Are they in the hospital?"

Lloyd snatches the phone out of my hand. THAT'S ENOUGH. And then it hits me, because he won't look at me, that it was him. He had all night to drive there and back.

YOU SAID YOU WERE GOING HOME. I WAS LOOKING FOR YOU. He spits out those words to the floor, and it's confirmed.

"Will they make it?" I say in the direction of the phone so Sax can hear me.

Lloyd hangs up the phone. YOUR DAD HAD THE BALLS TO POINT HIS SHOTGUN AT ME. I TOLD HIM THAT WHEN I SHOT HIM BETWEEN THE EYES. JUST TOOK THE GUN RIGHT OUT OF HIS SKINNY ARMS AND SAID, 'YOU DESERVE TO DIE, FUCKER.'

"My mother? Lloyd, my mother? And my sister? Lloyd?" I'm asking, but he's returned to the window and he holds back the curtain to look out.

I DIDN'T DO ANYTHING TO YOUR SISTER. SHE WASN'T HOME.

"But my mother?"

YOU'LL NEVER FORGIVE ME.

86

I can't tell you if I loved my father enough to mourn him or if it just makes me angry that it was his stupid guns that armed this maniac in my room. But my father didn't deserve to die this way.

87

"Shh . . . shh, Yoona, shh . . ." Faye's voice is far away, and I've fallen into a hole.

From somewhere above me, Lloyd is stomping his feet. Someone is shrieking, and if I could jump out of the window to get away from that sound, I would.

IT'S YOUR FAULT. YOU SAID YOU'D BE THERE. I WENT TO LAKEBURG TO TELL YOU WHAT SERENA TOLD ME. I HAD EVIDENCE THAT JAESUNG IS ALIVE. AND I WANTED TO TELL YOU. I WANTED YOU TO KNOW.

88

The fatigue fell like a heavy blanket over me at six each night without fail. I'd just gotten into bed with the folder the nurse had given me at the clinic. I'd been avoiding it, but now was the time. I had to see how I had to prepare. It took all my energy to force myself to open that folder. And then, just as I took out one of the forms inside, there was a knock on my door. I thought for a second it was Heather inviting me to the dining hall. I covered the folder with a blanket and opened the door.

Lloyd stood before me. He looked as if he hadn't showered in days. His shoulders were slumped, his face unshaven. He was wearing the same clothes he'd had on the last time I'd seen him, the same striped shirt and jeans. He probably didn't have many shirts or jeans in that backpack of his. I had never seen him use the laundry machines while he'd stayed with me.

"I have to talk to you," he said.

"Can't it be by phone?" I replied.

"I tried calling you, but it rang busy, and I got worried."

"I was talking to Willa."

"How's your mom?"

"Fine." I was surprised at how little I wanted to share with him and how little I cared about anything to do with him.

"Willa and your mom, they don't like me," he said.

"I've got a ton to do for my classes."

"Your dad say something to you about me? What about Willa? She was glaring at me in the waiting room as if she thinks I made your mom sick. She does, doesn't she? She thinks I did something to her?"

"No one's even thinking about you," I said and started closing the door.

He put his hand on the doorframe so I couldn't close it without smashing his fingers. "I called, Yoona. I just picked up the phone and called collect. Jaesung's father believes me. He's calling his brother in Korea about it. He sounded like he really appreciated what I said. He said it made sense." Lloyd's face was full of hope, and I wanted to believe him, but I knew he was lying.

"What evidence did you give him?" I said instead.

"He'd never heard the whole thing from me before. He said he was sorry about that. He wants to help me, and I think I got through to him. We didn't need evidence—I mean, I was an eyewitness to the whole conspiracy. I wasn't knocked out. I saw the whole thing with my eyes. I was there. They didn't count on that. And I don't care if they're following me. Let them. I've got Jaesung's father on my side now, and they can't follow everybody I tell. That's my plan: to tell everybody and not keep it secret. They can't shut me up. See, that's the part they were counting on, that I'd keep it a secret, but why should I? You get it?"

"He's going to look into it? What else did he say?"

"Can't I come in and talk about this? We had such a long conversation. I'm sitting in the phone booth at the library, and I was there until it closed, so it was really a long time. He left at one point and said he'd put the phone down, but he was still there, just had to take care of something, and I should keep talking because what I said was important, and it was good to have someone really take me seriously for once, you know?"

"I can't listen to this anymore. Did you spray-paint the shantytown houses?"

"Look, it was a lot of information. I get that. He was taking notes, he said. You know, so he wouldn't forget anything. He wanted all my information and yours. He wanted my address and my parents' phone number—so it would be an official report. We'd file it together—a lawsuit, an official complaint about the accident."

"A lawsuit?"

"Yes, don't you see? We're getting lawyers involved. That's what we're doing, and he's got the money to do it, and now we'll bring out the big guns to show them what they're dealing with. And if it's money they want in exchange for Jaesung, now they can get it. Jaesung's father said he'll pay anything to get Jaesung back, and I said I'd help him with that, and you would too. They just need to know we'd do it for real and hurry about getting him back. What do you think they're doing to him, Yoona?"

He was pounding on the frame of the door as he spoke, and it was unnerving me. It reminded me of the way my father would start his arguments, asking questions but not looking for answers. In fact, answers increased his rage. "I have to go," I said firmly and closed the door halfway.

He swayed from the door in dejection. "I can't believe you still don't believe me," he said. Then he leaned against the wall opposite my door and slid to a sitting position on the floor facing me and buried his face in his arms.

"You can't stay here," I said.

"That's what you think."

I closed the door to my room without another word.

I chucked the folder under my bed, turned out the light, and went to sleep. My watch said it was six forty-five. I woke to complete darkness. It was nearly ten o'clock. There were voices in the hall as people returned to their rooms. A few girls passed by when I opened my door. I heard one of them say, "Sorry," and saw her veer away, and then I saw beyond their feet that Lloyd was still camped out exactly where I'd left him. I shut and locked the door behind me before walking to the bathroom. When I returned, I stepped back over him, and he grabbed my foot. "Let go or I'll scream," I told him.

"You're going to regret this," he said.

Joanna came down the hall. "What's going on here?" she said.

Lloyd released my foot, and I shook my head at Joanna and escaped into my room. I heard her say something to him but couldn't make out the words, and then she must have continued down the hall.

89

Please stop that high-pitched sound. Is it Heather who's making that noise? Because Faye is beside me in this hole, holding me down in this room, when really the air outside is where I want to be. Winds. We loved the winds in Korea, didn't we, Jaesung? All I've ever done is try to keep my mother safe, and after all those years with my father, the illness in the hospital, when things were looking better for her, I bring this lunatic into her life. I wanted something for me, for once, for me. I wanted to love you, and this is what I did to my mother. Selfish, stupid, selfish, stupid, selfish, stupid. I take it back now. I wish I'd never met you. I wish I'd never met you and Lloyd. A hundred fists pummel my chest, with each crushing blow a shriek says, *My fault, my fault, my fault.*

90

It was Joanna who called me to her room the next afternoon. A man and a woman were in her doorway. Joanna ushered them into the hallway, where she made the introductions. "The dean's office notified Mr. and Mrs. Kang about the report I submitted yesterday with your complaint. Apparently, the Kangs had called the school asking for information about their son." The woman looked to be my mother's age but with thick foundation and powder. She was wearing a pink Chanel suit with pink pumps, as if dressed for a garden wedding. There was a corsage of pink roses and baby's breath on her lapel. The man hovered even though he didn't tower over her. It was his bent posture that made him seem to be looming. He had a thick, full head of wavy white hair.

"You're a friend of Lloyd's?" He nodded as if it would will me to nod in affirmation, which I felt compelled to do.

"We have to see him right away," he continued.

A group of boys and girls walked by, and we had to step aside for them. They were curious. I could tell by their stares. One of them was Daiyu, who ducked between two girls when our eyes met. I didn't understand why she didn't stop.

"I don't know where he is, I'm sorry," I said and saw them look at each other.

"How do you know our son?" Lloyd's father said.

"Where did you see him last?" the woman asked, and murmured to the man to wait.

"We have the word out to everybody to be on the lookout. We'll find him," Joanna said.

"I've told him to go back to New York," I said. "He probably will." I felt as though I had to reassure them somehow. I'd raised the alarm, but maybe he was driving back at this very moment. Lloyd's parents were whispering to each other. I saw Joanna peek at her wristwatch.

His mother finally turned to me, raising her hand to stop her husband from speaking. "The best thing to do if you see him is to call us." She searched in her bag, found an empty envelope, ripped it into two pieces, and wrote a number on each part. She handed one to me and the other to Joanna. "We've given our number to the dean's office too. Please call us as soon as you hear. We're at Creek Inn downtown."

Lloyd's father spoke. "We need to get him home."

"In Korea we hoped he'd make new friends," his mother said.

"What happened in the accident?" I said.

Lloyd's parents looked at each other again.

"I know he was in a car, and Jaesung was in a different one, ahead of Lloyd's, and Lloyd's car was hit by another car," I finished and waited.

Lloyd's father studied his feet and said, "He keeps saying that the boy, Jaesung, was in another car, but there was only one car. Somehow Lloyd must have been thrown from it, because the car was on fire by the time the fire trucks came."

A buzzing sound began in my brain.

Lloyd's father was still talking, still looking at his feet. "Lloyd called this boy's father two nights ago. That's how we knew he was up here. He told him that he had evidence that Jaesung was alive. Jaesung's father called us because he said Lloyd sounded confused. Said erratic nonsense things. Mr. Kim was very kind. The man's son has died, and he still has time to call me and apologize. It's all my fault for sending Lloyd to Korea. I knew the protests were happening. It wasn't—"

"We had to get him away from that girl from high school," Lloyd's mother said, a plea in her eyes.

"What girl?" I asked.

She shook her head. "It doesn't matter. He doesn't even mention her anymore. High school friend, that's all. Now all he talks about is Jaesung. Everything is about Jaesung. My poor son."

"Jaesung's father is sure he was in the same car?" I hardly recognized my voice. It was so small. It suddenly came crashing down on me. You were gone, gone, gone, and now you felt gone too. There was nothing I felt out there that was your life somewhere. There was emptiness in the pit of my stomach, emptiness and a buzzing, an unbearable persistent buzzing, as if a lightbulb above us were about to be extinguished.

"I've got to go," I said and didn't look to see their response. I'd known Lloyd's assessment of your father's response was off. It was too good to be true, too easy. You don't call up someone's father after he believes he saw his son's charred body and tell him that that was a mistake, that someone is fooling everyone.

Where could you be? I broke out in a cold sweat, this time the flu for certain. I crawled into bed.

91

WHAT THE FUCK IS WRONG WITH HER? IS SHE HURT? IS THE BABY OKAY? Lloyd is shouting and stomping around with his hands in his hair. Where are the guns?

Faye whispers, "Please, Yoona, please be quiet." She has her arms around me. Lloyd stands above us. "You've got to give her a minute," Faye says to him.

And that's when I realize what I have to do. The baby doesn't exist. Not now. It's up to me. If it wasn't for that report, Lloyd wouldn't know about it. But it helps me now. You help me now. This dream of Lloyd's. Even from this summer, our night together, from that I have this small possibility of saving Heather's and Faye's lives. I get to my feet.

92

Willa and I weren't allowed to have toys when we were children, but we could read as many books as we wanted. We were taken to the library and allowed to check out as many books as we could carry. Books were enough for Willa, but I wanted dolls. My father's chess set waited on the coffee table in the living room for me to play pretend with each night. The king and queen were my dolls. I moved them around the board, pretending they were two feuding families or a school yard full of children. My father insisted I learn chess if I was going to handle the pieces. I hated the game, especially the end game. It had to be to the death. That's the part I hated. The goal of the game was to kill. I squirmed in my seat at that part. In school I won tournaments against children older than I was. And then I quit. And I never played chess or pretended with the chess pieces again.

You and I never played chess or talked about it. I wonder if you knew the game. In chess, particularly effective in the end game, you can pin a piece to the king. Even the queen, the most powerful piece on the board, cannot move away if it means her king will be in check. A bishop or a rook, worth fewer points, can sacrifice itself, swap its death for the queen's death.

93

I woke from a deep sleep to knocking. Daiyu was at my door. "Oh, Yoona," she said. It was quiet in the hall, and from the hall window, I could see it was late, because it was very dark outside. Faye and Heather were with her.

"Go ahead," Heather said.

"What's going on?" I rubbed my eyes. "Don't come too close, it's the flu," I murmured, but Daiyu didn't answer.

Heather spoke. "Daiyu told Lloyd that you called his parents and that they're here on campus, and he got really mad and said he was going to crash his car because he's never going back to New York with them."

Daiyu looked down at her sneakered feet.

"I'm sorry, Yoona. He asked me if I'd seen you, and I told him no at first, but then he said I was lying, so I had to tell him I'd seen you with his parents. They were his parents, weren't they? Lloyd looks just like his father except for the white hair."

I felt like I was in my own personal bubble, filling up with fog. I told my friends what Lloyd's parents had said. I could see, even in my foggy bubble, that they were suddenly frightened of him.

"You can't let him stay in your room anymore," Faye said to Daiyu, and Daiyu nodded.

"He obsesses about people: the girl from his high school, and Jaesung, and now you," Daiyu said to me.

Faye said, "Everything he's said to us is a lie."

94

When Tuesday came around, I called my mother and told her I would not be home for fall break. I told her I had too many assignments overdue. That part was true. I didn't tell her I'd be taking a bus in the opposite direction on that Friday and couldn't quite manage turning around and being on the bus for another six hours that same day to go to Lakeburg for the long weekend. I saw it as a fresh start.

I went by Professor Wong's office later that day, and he waved me in. Did I tell you he looked as if he was only a few years older than us? He wore long gym shorts most days, even when it was cold, and flip-flops and long-sleeved T-shirts with video game graphics on them. Today it was Space Invaders. It was easy to talk to him because he seemed less formal than the other professors on campus. He told us to call him Julian, so when I walked in I said, "I'm sorry, Julian, I'll get you two papers before I leave for break."

He reclined in his beat-up leather desk chair, his hands behind his head. "Things overwhelming you?"

I tapped the edge of his desk, which had piles of paper on it as if they'd been dumped there. I'd had to walk around short pillars of stacked books on the floor. His office looked as if he'd moved in without boxes and deposited things in a hurry. "There's a lot going on."

"I know how it can be. I was given a warning after my first semester." He straightened up in his chair again and leaned forward, his elbows on piles of paper.

"What happened to you?" I asked.

"I wasn't ready for college. High school had been intense. Racing to the end of it. A year between was what I needed. Maybe you should consider it."

"It's not the workload."

"Well, okay, talk to me. Not the workload—is it the social scene?"

"Is there any reason the Chun regime would kidnap an American student?"

"You're talking South Korea, President Chun?" He leaned back again, his hands on the armrests this time.

"I'm saying what would be the point?"

"If the student is thought to be a spy, North Korea might kidnap people they think are spies. Well, South Korean spies."

Lloyd was right. Could it be North Korea who took you? "If they thought he was South Korean because he's Korean American. I mean he was born here in the States, but he looks Korean. Speaks Korean."

"It's not likely, because what would be the motive? As soon as they found out, they'd give him back. Kim Il Sung doesn't want an all-out war with the United States, and with all the troops at the DMZ, South Korea would love an excuse to start one."

"They'd give him back? Say it was a mistake?" I pressed him for more.

"It'd be pretty fast. If it was a mistake, they'd know immediately. They've kidnapped fishermen and South Koreans, but an American citizen? It wouldn't be in their best interest to try something like that." Julian began shuffling the papers on his desk and looked as if he'd like to read a few of them at that very moment.

"So you think it couldn't happen." I let out a breath.

"Not really," he said and seemed satisfied that he'd put his papers in order. He looked up at me.

"Is there anyone you'd call to find out?"

"Is this about political persecution of journalists in Korea? Are you focusing on KBS and the National Security Law?"

"Maybe."

"You can't get much information about the Blue House. Maybe in a few years."

"So you're saying there isn't any reason to lie about an American student if anything happened to him in Korea?"

"You okay, Yoona? You should take a seat."

I stayed on my feet. "Thanks, but I've got to go."

"I'm not one of those who stick to a tight schedule. I told everyone in class I want six papers this semester in addition to the final. If you need more time for these two, you'll just have to do a lot of work at the end of the semester. We're going to get to more censorship issues as the semester goes on, so maybe you'll want to write about a topic you can find more information on then. Don't sweat it. I mean it, okay?"

I nodded and turned to leave.

"I'll see you in class tomorrow, right?" he called after me.

I told him I would be there, but it was an automatic response. Julian had said there was no chance you were kidnapped, and I believed him. I'd hoped he'd convince me that Chun or Kim Il Sung, one of them, had taken you. And offer a way to find you.

95

I called the number on my ripped piece of envelope, and Lloyd's father answered. I told him Lloyd was headed back to New York, threatening to kill himself on the way but heading back. He thanked me and hung up without another word.

Lloyd was in my room on Wednesday afternoon, sitting on my bed. He had a light-blue folder on his lap. It was familiar, but I couldn't remember why.

"You should be more careful about locking your door," he said, answering the question I was about to shout at him. Something about him made me nervous. It was like that time in the mandu shop when he smashed that cup. He swept his arm across my bedside table and knocked the lamp to the floor, the phone and the receiver, knocking everything off, the mug, a spoon. I steeled myself. *Not in my room*, I thought, not the way my father raged at home, but this time I was more nervous than when I'd been firm with him at my house. This time I stayed quiet and let him talk. All about how much he trusted me. Had trusted me. Had never thought I'd betray him this way. That he'd gone with me to my parents' house and had been polite. Not let on all the things I'd told him about them. But not me. Me, I'd told his parents all the things he'd said. I'd made them think he was crazy. I'd told Faye and Daiyu and Heather that he was crazy. He knew because they wouldn't let him in their rooms anymore, and he knew because they walked away when he approached them.

"Were there ever people following you?" I said. "Was any of it true? Is Jaesung alive?" I could hardly get your name out.

"How can you ask me that?" he said, and he fell on his knees and pulled me down to the floor beside him. "Yoona, you and Jaesung, you've been the only two people in the world who I knew were my friends. True friends. I've never lied to you. I'd never lie to you. I mean, I don't know what's happened between us. I've been trying to figure it out, but you just changed."

I didn't know what to say. I pulled my hands away and began righting the things he'd upended. I put the receiver back on the phone, but left it on the floor, because he reached for my hands again. I had to figure out a way to get him out of my room.

"Your parents want to help you," I said.

"My parents? Are you kidding me? They want to lock me up."

This time I was firm. Here was my opening. "They're really worried about you. Lloyd, you need to see your doctor and get help."

"Are you really pregnant with Jaesung's baby?" he said. Half his breath must have been held as he spoke. His heart must have felt to him as if it had paused. I saw the stillness. He waited for confirmation.

I had to protect October 22.

He opened the folder. "You wanted official, I got official—just not about Jaesung. The clinic is easy to break into."

I saw my name at the top of the document.

"Don't you see?" he continued. "They'll never win now. Even though they have Jaesung, they'll never have his son."

I backed away from him. "I'm calling the police."

"The love you two had was so powerful you made a new life. Even when they tried to stop him, they couldn't, don't you see? And when he's released, he'll have this child to come home to. Don't you see?"

"That's confidential, Lloyd. It's illegal to look at someone's files."

"You're in shock, and they've convinced you—when did you find out? Is this the reason why you've shut me out? Because I'm Jaesung's best friend, and you want to pretend this baby isn't real? It all makes sense now. Your feelings for me changed because they convinced you not to have this baby. They turned you against me. Who was it? Was it your father? Your mother? Willa. It was Willa, wasn't it?"

"No, no, no, no, no," I repeated. I walked to the door and held it open. It had worked before, and I was counting on it again. I had to get him out of my room. A week, my head reminded me. Seven days and I wouldn't be standing on this precipice anymore.

"If we make an announcement, a public one, they'll know Jaesung has a son," he said.

"Get out, Lloyd."

"What if I convince Willa and your mom? Your dad too, because they'd want a grandchild if they really thought about it. What if I convince them that you must have this baby?"

"That's not going to change my mind," I said. "Get out or I'll call campus police."

"Daiyu and Heather? They must have known all along. That's what Faye meant when she said you had big decisions to make. That's what Serena said when she said you were switching majors. She meant this. She meant you were going to be a mother. You're having Jaesung's child." He jumped up and down in place, spilling the contents of the folder to the floor. He swung his arms as if he were punching ghosts. "What will you name him? It can't be too close to Jaesung's name, but maybe he'll look like him, and I'll take care of him. I'd be his godfather, of course, until Jaesung comes back. He'll be so happy, and he'll know we never forgot about him. We kept his memory alive. I'll tell his son all about the things we did over the summer, how great his father—"

"Lloyd, what about me?" I was becoming furious. "This is about me. It's happening to me. Inside my body, Lloyd. I'm not doing it. I can't do it. I won't ruin my life."

"You?" He stared at me. "Is that what this is about? You're only thinking about you? I'm not going to let you kill Jaesung's child. No one is going to hurt Jaesung ever again." He lunged at me but then jerked back like a dog on a leash, turned, and ran out of the room.

I was shaking and breathing hard. I ran to the bathroom and threw up. With my head hanging over the toilet, I knew I would never make it to the clinic. I just didn't know how it would happen.

I missed the next two days of classes, going only to the dining hall or food truck and then returning to my room, nervous about running into Lloyd on campus. I finished two papers. And now I had to deliver one to Professor Wong's office. It was six forty-five on Friday, and most students were in the dining hall for dinner. Leaves had fallen almost overnight, blanketing the grass in rusty shades, and it was dark, dark as the middle of the night. An owl hooted somewhere in a tree behind me. An oddly persistent owl whose hoot became a wolf's howl. It was an eerie sound, and when I looked at the expanse of the empty quad I had to traverse, I had second thoughts about delivering my essay. In the next minute, the wolf was in front of me on the walkway. Lloyd howled, his hands in his pockets, wearing a long gray coat. I turned around and began walking back to my room, but he ran around to face me from that side. So I turned again, and this time he ran right up to me, and I flinched.

"I'm not going to hurt you," he said.

I sucked in my breath and tried to appear as if he didn't rattle me. "I'm busy, Lloyd."

He peered at me. I held up my hand to shield myself. He looked ecstatic, with flushed cheeks and a smile that couldn't contain his teeth. I attempted to walk around him, but he mirrored my steps and remained an obstacle, hopping in some sort of wild dance.

"Leave me alone," I said.

"Why should I?"

"I'll scream."

"Go ahead."

"I have to hand in these papers."

"I don't like the way that Professor Wong looks at you."

"Get out of my way, Lloyd."

"Not until you cancel your appointment in Scranton."

"How do you know about that?" I hadn't told anyone, not Serena, not Heather or Faye or Daiyu.

"You just told me," he said. He laughed up at the sky.

I tried again to walk past him, but he moved with me and grabbed at my arms, which I pulled out of his grasp. "You disgust me, you know that?"

I was aware of how ridiculous we looked, twisting as we did, in one direction and then the next, but I had to get away from him. I fought the impulse to lose control entirely.

"It could be mine. What if it's mine?" he taunted.

That sent ice down my throat. And I forced myself to talk to him. "Listen to me, Lloyd. Lloyd Kang, are you listening to me?"

He looked expectantly into my eyes. He was pleased with himself. "I'm all yours," he said. "It could be mine, there's a chance. You have to admit there's a chance."

"We never came close to it, Lloyd. I love Jaesung."

"See? You think he's still alive." He smiled triumphantly.

"Stop saying it could be yours."

"There was that one night, remember? You were drunk, my god, so drunk, and so sad. You were so sad and lonely. You said I should stay because you didn't want to be alone. You were soft and warm, and it was such a cold night, no heat in the room, remember, and we even talked about how guilty we felt, you know, afterward, about Jaesung. You told me about your dad. It makes sense, but don't worry, I'll explain to Jaesung how it happened. I don't love you, so that's okay—you're not my type, honestly. I need a much older woman, and he knows that. Miss Ahn on the tour, she liked me. Jaesung knew about that. So he'll forgive us. We were trying to help him, and we didn't mean any of it, just like that."

"It's not yours in any way. It can't be."

"Well, that clears it up. It said so in your file, but, then again, it's an approximation. Since you're nauseous, the baby doesn't have the placenta to feed off of yet, so that could put you at six weeks, which might make me the father."

"Still wouldn't work. Forget it. Do the math."

"You're making me suffer, but that's okay. That's what you do. You made Jaesung suffer, and now you're making me. I forgive you. Look, we could raise the baby here. Until we find Jaesung, of course. My parents would help us with money. My mother cried. I called her from Daiyu's room, and she said she wants to help us raise this baby. I've never heard her as excited about anything before. I think this baby is going to change everything." He opened his arms. "I've been thinking it over, and my plan would work. Of course, if the baby is Jaesung's, I'd step aside. He'd want me to. But if it's mine, then he'd have to step aside. And after all he's been through, he might prefer if I raise the baby anyway. I'm better for this. He's going to be a world leader, but I could be his adviser, part-time. Being a father is a full-time job. I'd make him understand, and even if it was his child, maybe he'd let me. I think he would. The more I think about it. He'd say, you're the only one who didn't give up on me. You can have this child."

I couldn't hear any more of this. He was crazy.

I hadn't seen how delusional he was before. He wasn't going to go away. Every few feet in this part of the quadrangle, there was a blue light on a lamp pole marking the emergency telephones. I was close to one. "I'm warning you."

"You mean, kill our baby."

"It's not yours."

"So you admit it's a baby?"

"No, it's not. It's none of your business. I can't."

"We have to be saved from ourselves sometimes, Yoona."

"I'll cancel my appointment in Scranton. I'm going home first." The lie came as a desperate attempt to get away from him.

"I don't believe you."

I felt a surge of hysteria rising in me, and I ran, and he came after me. I saw, out of the side of my eyes, a pole with a blue light at the top, and I ran toward it. But before I got there, I saw a couple of students with blue T-shirts on standing near a building, so I changed direction and ran toward them. I could hear Lloyd behind me. I stopped in front of the pair.

"What's going on here?" the girl said.

"He's threatening me," I answered, my hands on my knees. I bent forward to try to catch my breath.

"I'm going to be the father to her baby," he yelled out, and the smile on his face transformed it into something grotesque.

"It doesn't matter who you are if you're trying to hurt her," she said.

"Yeah? You think I want to hurt my baby?" Lloyd lurched toward her. She stood her ground and stared at him, ignoring his stance.

"Back up," the boy said and took a step toward Lloyd. Lloyd seemed startled at his presence, as if he hadn't registered another person had been there all along. The girl unclipped the walkie-talkie on her hip and requested backup. The sound of static and an official-sounding woman's voice saying, "Situation?" seemed to startle Lloyd even more.

"You'll regret this. I know who you are," he shouted at the girl. Then he raised a fist toward the boy and said, "You too." The boy didn't flinch, and Lloyd backed away, spinning around on his heels and running diagonally through the quad. Relief rose in tears to my eyes as he disappeared into the distance.

"You okay?" the boy asked.

"Thank you," I said.

"You should report him," the girl said.

96

"You're right. We have to save the baby," I tell Lloyd and shake Faye off. Faye looks at me with hurt in her eyes.

YOU'RE NOT MAD ABOUT YOUR MOTHER?

I look at him the way I've been trained to look at my father. "You went all the way to Lakeburg like you did that time you helped me, when my mom was in the hospital. I was thinking that was really nice of you to do that. Go all the way there even when I treated you horribly. Been thinking you were always a good friend. Good friend to Jaesung. Good friend to me. You're right—I cut and run all the time. Too much, really. Even with this pregnancy. Hard when I feel so sick all the time, you know? Is the car ready? Call Sax back and tell him we're in a hurry. I have to use the bathroom. One of the problems with being pregnant."

"Don't, Yoona, don't do this," Faye pleads.

THE BATHROOM? IS THAT SOME SORT OF TRICK?

"I'll use the bathroom far away from here once we have the car and the money. It was my parents who really wanted me not to have this baby. You took care of that problem, so I can deal with it now. You went overboard, like you do, but you saved me, really."

YOU THINK I SAVED YOU?

"We have to hurry now if it's going to work."

WHAT'S GOING TO WORK?

"I didn't go home because they gave me hell on the phone about it. Typical." As I talk, I have to speak in a low voice. My head is pounding, a dozen microscopic hammers battering me in different tempos inside.

"Look out the window and see what they're doing out there. I'll get the girls ready."

He looks confused.

"Honestly, that temporary FBI thing Sax said sounds like a lie. Serena said something about it, but it sounded fake."

SERENA'S A BITCH.

"We have to bring them both, don't you think? We don't know who we will have to use to get through whatever roadblock they'll set up. You know they'll try once we're out of the building. Maybe we'll need Serena too. Maybe we should stop by her dorm, if they haven't evacuated the campus."

BUT HE SAID PRESIDENT REAGAN IS GOING TO FREE JAESUNG.

"Did he? I didn't hear that. I heard some bullshit about you being made part of the FBI."

185

"Yoona, why are you saying that? She's wrong, Lloyd. Don't listen to her." Faye pulls at my arm.

"Jaesung always said you were gullible. Really smart but gullible," I tell him.

Lloyd looks from me to Faye. Then he looks down at the handgun, his thumb caressing the handle.

"What are you doing, Yoona?" Faye hisses.

Lloyd looks straight at me, and I don't blink. DON'T LET THEM GET CLOSE TO THE DOOR OR ELSE THEY'LL ESCAPE. YOU REALLY THINK HE'S LYING? There's a flicker of the old Lloyd who came to Weston a month ago.

"Is the car ready?" I say.

Lloyd backs up to the window, and when he turns his head, I point to Heather for Faye to help her up.

I CAN SEE THE VAN. THEY'RE FILLING IT WITH BRIEFCASES. IT MUST BE THE MONEY. THE MAN WITH THE RED HAT IS GONE.

"See? Sax is trying to make sure you feel safe," I say, and I've got my arm around Heather now, and I motion Faye to follow with a finger to my mouth signaling her to be quiet. Faye takes Heather's arm, and Heather whimpers in pain. We make our way to the door.

IT'S A CHEVY LIKE MY DAD HAS. I'LL TELL SAX TO PUT A MEDICAL KIT IN FOR HEATHER. YOU'RE RIGHT—WE'LL NEED HER.

I nudge the desk with my hip and shove it over with my free hand. Just a few more steps and we'll be at the door.

97

Lloyd picks up the phone with a smile on his face, as if a load is off his shoulders. I'M GOING TO TAKE CARE OF EVERYTHING, he tells me. Into the phone, he shouts, YOU TRIED TO FOOL ME WITH THAT TEMPORARY FBI SHIT, SAX. BUT WE DIDN'T FALL FOR IT.

"Who's 'we,' Lloyd? Who didn't fall for what?"

'WE' MEANS ME AND YOONA. WE HAVE PLANS. IT'S GOING TO BE ALL RIGHT NOW. TELL PRESIDENT REAGAN TO INFORM CHUN DOO HWAN AND KIM IL SUNG THAT WE HAVE JAESUNG KIM'S BABY. THEY HAVE TO FREE HIM. HE'S AN AMERICAN. AND, IF WE HAVE TO, WE'LL EXPOSE THE KCIA SPY WHO IS WITH HIM. I'M NOT GOING TO LET MY BEST FRIEND SUFFER BECAUSE OF HIM.

"Stay in front of me," I tell Faye as loudly as I can manage with my stomach in knots and nausea rising in my throat. "Come on, Heather, a little further."

"Yoona, what are you doing?" Faye says and refuses to move.

"Open the door, Faye," I tell her. "I got Heather." We pivot so we are sideways to Lloyd. And she uses her right hand to open the door. I can feel cool air. "Move toward it, that's right," I continue.

DON'T GO YET, YOONA. SAX SAYS FIVE MINUTES. Lloyd's voice is steady.

"Just seeing if anyone is in the hall," I tell him without looking back.

BUT THEN THEY CAN ESCAPE. YOU DON'T KNOW, BUT—STOP, CLOSE THE DOOR.

"Now," I say to Faye. I push Heather toward the door so she stumbles into Faye, who is now in the hallway.

I'LL BLOW A HOLE STRAIGHT THROUGH ALL OF YOU.

But I've made sure I'm between the shotgun and Heather, so when we both stop at the sound of his words, he would have to shoot through me to kill her, which he's saying he's going to do—my brain processes this as if it can't accept self-sacrifice and refuses to move my feet when Heather takes another step. I don't follow, and she's in his range now.

"Lloyd, Lloyd, don't do it. Let's talk it over." Detective Sax's tiny voice comes through the phone on the floor as Lloyd repositions his grip on the shotgun, and it breaks my paralysis. I step closer to Heather.

Heather and Faye are pinned to me.

That's when Lloyd says what I've been counting on him to say—some unconscious part of me has known all along. MOVE OUT OF THE WAY, YOONA.

"Hold on, Lloyd, slow down. Don't do anything to ruin our deal. The car is ready outside now. It's right there, Lloyd," Sax urges.

YOONA IS GOING TO MAKE ME KILL HER AND JAESUNG'S BABY. HOW CAN I STOP HER?

"You can't." I speak to him over my shoulder.

A few more steps. If Lloyd pulls that trigger, we're all doomed. But I know he won't shoot your baby.

"Keep going," I tell my friends and turn to face Lloyd again.

98

WHY ARE YOU DOING THIS, YOONA? OUR CAR IS DOWNSTAIRS. WE CAN GO TO THE AIRPORT AND GET ON A PLANE. PRESIDENT REAGAN IS WAITING FOR US. WE CAN FREE JAESUNG. YOU AND I CAN SEE HIM AGAIN.

"You don't have proof, Lloyd." I feel a calm spread through me. Is this what the students felt before they lit themselves on fire? Did you feel this when the other car collided into you? The door is still open, but my friends have gone through. "Give yourself up," I tell Lloyd.

BUT WE'VE GOTTEN WHAT WE WANT.

"I don't care what you do to me—I'm walking out right now."

SERENA HAD A FAX FROM THE DIRECTOR OF THE KCIA. IT'S PROOF, ASK HIM—ASK SAX TO SEARCH HER ROOM. I TRIED TO GET HER TO SHOW IT TO ME, BUT SHE WOULDN'T. I'M SORRY I HAD TO SHOOT HER. I'M REALLY SORRY. YOONA, PLEASE. HE'S ALIVE. THE FAX SAYS HE'S A PRISONER IN NORTH KOREA. THE STATE DEPARTMENT KNOWS ABOUT HIM. THEY KNOW, AND THEY'RE GOING TO LET HIM ROT THERE. WE'RE SO

CLOSE. THIS IS OUR REVOLUTION, YOONA. WE'VE DONE IT. THE SMALL REVOLUTIONS MAKE THE WAY FOR THE BIG ONES. REMEMBER WHAT JAESUNG SAID ABOUT SMALL REVOLUTIONS. THIS IS OUR REVOLUTION, YOONA. DON'T GIVE UP ON HIM NOW. HOW CAN YOU GIVE UP ON HIM NOW? I DID ALL THIS FOR HIM, FOR YOU.

Lloyd is talking so fast I can hardly understand what he's saying. The room begins to spin, a record that is on fast-forward. What you said was there were many paths to revolution. What would you say about what Lloyd is doing here now?

YOU KNOW I HAD TO DO IT. SERENA IM IS A SPY. WHAT MUSICAL PRODIGY TAKES A YEAR OFF TO GO TO A CRAPPY SCHOOL LIKE WESTON? IT DOESN'T HAVE A MUSIC PROGRAM. I KNEW HER STORY WAS FULL OF SHIT. DID YOU EVER HEAR HER PLAY THE CELLO? EVER? SHE WAS LURING YOU TO NEW YORK WITH THAT INTERVIEW TO KIDNAP YOU. I MADE IT QUICK, FOR YOUR SAKE. ONE SHOT, LIKE ALL THOSE SPIES DO IT.

Serena's face hovers before my eyes. "You and me, we're not so different," she used to say. "Okay, we are, but not really, not at our core."

"Why didn't anyone hear you shoot her, Lloyd?" I try to hold on to logic. I can't believe what he's saying. Not Serena too. There's no bottom to this falling nightmare. Lloyd's voice goes on and on.

IT WAS HER FATHER'S FRIEND. SHE SAID HE WORKED FOR THE KCIA AND GOT HOLD OF AN INTEROFFICE MEMO. THAT'S WHAT I WAS TRYING TO FIND. I ONLY MEANT TO SCARE HER WITH THE GUN. I MEANT TO MAKE HER GIVE ME THE FAX OF THAT MEMO, BUT SHE SAID I WAS CRAZY. SHE SAID IF YOU WERE PREGNANT, THEN I MUST HAVE RAPED YOU, AND I TOLD HER NOT TO SPREAD LIES. BUT SHE WAS GOING TO. SHE WAS. I HAD TO STOP HER. JAESUNG WOULD HATE ME. SHE WOULDN'T SHUT UP. I HAD TO SHUT HER UP. SHE WOULDN'T SHOW ME THE FAX. SO I HAD TO FORCE HER. YOU UNDERSTAND I DID IT FOR JAESUNG. FOR YOU. WE COULD USE THAT FAX TO PROVE THEY KNEW. THE STATE DEPARTMENT KNEW ABOUT HIM.

99

Lloyd's voice is babble now, nonsensical babble. So much gone. Everyone gone. And I'm at the center of it. Me. Me. Me. What have I done?

100

"Yoona." It's your voice calling to me. "Get up."

101

I'm kneeling on the floor. I don't remember how I came to be on the floor. I stand up. "You have a memo?" I can hear my voice, and it's shaky. Lloyd still has the shotgun pointing in my direction, but he's lowered it.

THE ONLY THING THAT MAKES SENSE IS THAT TONGSU CHO MUST HAVE BEEN A NORTH KOREAN SPY. I REMEMBER NOW THERE WAS THE SMELL OF FISH. WE WERE DRIVING TO THE DOCKS. JAESUNG WAS KID-NAPPED. SHIT, HE PROBABLY AGREED TO HELP UNIFY THE COUNTRY BY WORKING WITH THE NORTH. BUT HE MUST HAVE CHANGED HIS MIND ONCE HE GOT THERE. HE DIDN'T KNOW WHAT IT WOULD BE LIKE. THE MEMO SAYS HE'S IN PRISON. IF HE WANTED TO GO THERE TO HELP, WHY WOULD THEY PUT HIM IN PRISON, YOONA?

"Show it to me, Lloyd."

I THOUGHT YOU AND I COULD GO BACK TO HER ROOM AND SEARCH IT FOR THE ACTUAL MEMO. IF YOU JUST LISTENED TO ME, I WOULDN'T HAVE FORCED DAIYU TO COME. I WOULDN'T HAVE MADE HEATHER AND FAYE COME IN HERE. BUT YOU WOULDN'T EVEN TALK TO ME. DO YOU KNOW HOW THAT MADE ME FEEL? LOOK WHAT I BOUGHT—I WANTED

TO THINK IT COULD BE OUR BABY. ALL OF OURS. WE WERE THREE—A
TEAM IN KOREA, WEREN'T WE?

"Let her go, Lloyd." Sax's voice comes through a bullhorn.

JESUS, WHAT THE FUCK. Lloyd lurches to the window and pulls
aside the curtain, peers outside. It's the farthest he's opened the curtain,
and sunlight is streaming in, the mute October light of afternoon. Is it
afternoon already? My abdomen aches, and I think I'm so past wanting
to pee that I'm cramping. Lloyd rushes to pick up the phone and shouts
into it. NOW YOU HAVE THE GIRLS. WHERE'S THE CAR?

"It's over, Lloyd. Let the girl go." Sax continues to use the bullhorn.

YOONA, TELL HIM YOU WANT A CAR.

"Ask him for the memo," I tell him from the doorway.

OKAY, OKAY, WAIT. He holds the phone back up to his ear. ARE
YOU THERE? IN SERENA'S ROOM THERE'S A MEMO FROM THE STATE
DEPARTMENT. TELL YOONA YOU FOUND IT. He motions for me to come
to the phone, but I don't move from the doorway.

102

Sax's voice comes through the bullhorn, distorted at the end. "Come
on, Lloyd. We've searched the entire room, and there's no memo. You've
got to save yourself while you still have time. I can help you, but not for
much longer. Give me a chance to help you, Lloyd."

Lloyd holds his free hand up, covers his ear. His eyes are frantic. YOONA,
YOU HAVE TO BELIEVE ME. SAX DOESN'T KNOW WHAT THE MEMO LOOKS LIKE.
HE WOULDN'T KNOW A CONSPIRACY IF IT HIT HIM OVER THE HEAD.

"You're pointing a gun at me, Lloyd."

WHAT, THIS? He drops the gun, and it bounces on the floor once
before lying there. THIS WAS THE ONLY WAY.

"Lloyd."

His hands are open and empty. YOU WOULDN'T FUCKING TALK TO ME. I FOUND THE MEMO. I FOUND OUT SERENA WAS A SPY. I FOUND JAESUNG. ME, I FOUND HIM ALL BY MYSELF, BECAUSE YOU STOPPED TRYING. WHY DON'T YOU BELIEVE ME?

"You've lied from the beginning."

I KNOW, I KNOW. BUT THEY WERE IN OUR WAY—DON'T YOU SEE THAT? THEY'VE ALL BEEN IN OUR WAY. HOW CAN WE SAVE JAESUNG IF WE'RE NOT ABLE TO DO THE HARD THINGS? HE WAS RIGHT ABOUT THAT PART. YOU KNOW HE WAS RIGHT.

Something suddenly occurs to him. He shakes his head as if he's emerged from being under water. IF YOU THINK I'M GOING TO LET YOU WALK AWAY BEFORE I GIVE YOU THIS . . .

He inserts his hand into his inside coat pocket, at the chest. When his hand emerges, I think it'll be another gun. My father had a series of pistols. I flinch.

I hear a click, but nothing happens. Sunlight warms the room. Lloyd seems oblivious to it. He's silhouetted with his back to the window, and his hand emerges from his coat pocket. In one motion, he unfurls pale-blue infants' footed pajamas with a tag dangling from the sleeve. IF WE COULD JUST FREE HIM, HE COULD SEE THIS. LOOK, IT HAS SNAPS. YOU CAN SNAP IT TOGETHER LIKE THIS.

The blue footie hangs from Lloyd's hand, and his fingers rub one of a row of snap buttons that run down the baby pajamas. WE CAN GET HIM OUT. I PROMISE YOU HE'S ALIVE.

I don't imagine you outside the cab window anymore. Instead you're in a prison without windows, and you don't believe I'm coming for you. Your shoulders slump, your head bends to your chest, and your feet are bare. I see Lloyd and myself, maybe a baby in my arms, bursting into your prison cell. *You didn't forget,* you'd say.

"Wait," I call out.

103

He shoots me. And then there's the sound of voices and sirens, and I feel cold air, as if it's winter and I'm in a snowstorm. But I'm flat on the floor and above me is the white ceiling. Suddenly, I'm wrapped in a sheet, and hands hoist me up, and then the sun is in my eyes, and the rays are strong like when we were in Korea, pressing down on our heads. Something tells me to turn my head to the left, and I hear your voice. Just like the last time I saw you, you're saying, "Wait." And then you're here. Your face floats above me, and you say, "I told you I'd see you soon," and I can't believe it's really you. Lloyd had me convinced you were in a North Korean prison but here you are. How did you get here?

People crowd in, and you're pushed away, and I say, "Don't leave me," but they're prodding and pulling at each other, and you disappear from view. And then for a long moment there's silence, which makes me think I've lost my hearing. And then someone says, "Watch out," and there is another explosion of gunfire, but this time many bursts, as if I were sitting too close to fireworks on the Fourth of July. The floor vibrates, and I feel rather than see Lloyd disappear from this life. I say, "Wait, you were right, Lloyd," but he's gone. And I hear someone say, "That was close. We thought he was down. Everyone thought it was over. Who knew he would still try, even in that state, to shoot the girl?"

Which girl? Where are Faye and Heather?

"One, two, three, lift," someone says by my side, and I'm suddenly on a stretcher. Beyond is the face of a kind woman who looks like our postal carrier in Lakeburg, who says, "You're going to be all right."

"Heather, Faye?" I ask.

"They're fine." She's sticking a needle into my arm.

"Could you find Jaesung for me? He was just here a minute ago."

"The detectives will answer all your questions, don't worry, honey," she replies and pulls a blanket tight over me and tucks it under the stretcher. I tell her I have to see you, but she and others are rushing me downstairs now, and the stretcher sways from side to side. "Go back," I tell them. "He doesn't know where you're taking me."

"Shh . . . ," the woman coos to me. "There's no one by that name. Close your eyes and count backward from ten. I promise you it'll be all right."

104

The finality of her words comes crashing down around me. No one by that name. I can't trust my own eyes anymore. Didn't I see you a minute ago? Or is Lloyd right about you? Are you in a prison in North Korea? The concrete walls, the iron bars, the floor stained with blood and shit and hopelessness—did you shake those bars in despair? What have they been doing to you? Then all of a sudden I remember again your face outside the window of a cab in Seoul, your hand on the edge of the door, your beautifully imperfect finger. A voice in my head—did it know the future?—shouts at me, *Get out of the car right now. Open the door. Tell him you don't want to leave yet.*

And you said, "I'll see you soon."

There's a rush of air. We're outside, and there's the sound of car engines starting up around us, like when I saw you last in Seoul. Lloyd is gone, I have no doubts about that. But you? Why does it feel like a promise even after all this? I'll see you soon.

ACKNOWLEDGMENTS

Timing has been a significant factor in the publication of this book. The perfect agent for me, the perfect editor, along with friends (who provided the perfect support for me) came into my life at the perfect moment. Even my family cooperated in spectacular fashion. As this manuscript goes into production, I'm deeply grateful to the following:

My husband and our daughters; my teaching partner and confidant, Patricia Dunn; my lovely agent, Cynthia Manson; and my brilliant editor, Vivian Lee.

Thanks to Dara Kaye, Janice Lee, Al Woodworth, Marlene Kelly, Merideth Mulroney, Emily Mahon, Dan Byrne, and Gabriella Dumpit.

I couldn't have written this book without Kate Brandt, Gloria Hatrick, Deborah Zoe Laufer, Maria Maldonado, Kim Lopp Manocherian, Alexandra Soiseth, Katharine Houghton, Gwendolen Gross, and their families.

Thank you to my own family, particularly Cathy and Henry Byon, and their children and spouses (especially Juyeon Byon). Many of your stories and questions made their way into this story.

To Nancee Adams, Joy Castro, Steve Edwards, Susan Greenberg, Julie Iromuanya, Jennifer Manocherian, Kreesan Pillay, Alan Russell, the fabulous Sarah Lawrence College community, the Saturday Fantastics, and the Thursday group at the Scarsdale Public Library—I'll always be grateful.

For their friendship and inspiration, thanks go to Mary-Kim Arnold, Kathy Fish, Michael A. Horowitz, Ed Park, Linda Rodriguez, Matthew Salesses, Gabriel Spera, and Peter Tieryas, to name a few.

Last but not least, I want to thank those who seemed to believe in me long before I did: my childhood teachers Grace Dorman, Donald Mudge, Myron Rew, and Dwight Willson. I also want to thank my dear old friend Theresa Choh-Lee and her husband, H. J. Lee, who said I'd better get my novel published so they could organize a reading for me (I'm ready!), and a fellow student in a writing class I took in New York City years ago, who told me once he'd see my book in a shop window someday. I never forgot.

ABOUT THE AUTHOR

Photo © Janice Chung

Jimin Han received her MFA at Sarah Lawrence College and her BA from Cornell University. Her work appears in NPR's *Weekend America*, *Entropy*, the *Rumpus*, *HTMLGiant*, *The Good Men Project*, *Kartika Review*, *The NuyorAsian Anthology*, and KoreanAmericanStory.org, among others. She teaches at Sarah Lawrence College's Writing Institute and lives outside New York City with her husband and children.